Conditions

by

Skye Mueller

Cover Art by *Tina Lynn Stout*

The Wild Rose Press, Inc.
PO Box 708
Adams Basin, NY 14410-0708
Visit us at www.thewildrosepress.com

Publishing History
First Edition, 2025
Trade Paperback Print ISBN 978-1-5092-6409-4
Digital ISBN 978-1-5092-6410-0

Published in the United States of America

Dedication

For my family, your support means everything.

Chapter One

The balmy evening Summer Halley chose to put off her paperwork and leave the clinic early was the evening that altered the carefully reconstructed course of her life.

The emergence of a looming shadow that fell into step behind her didn't necessarily make her pause. After all, she'd been followed by faceless associates before—though it had, admittedly, been quite a long time since the last incident.

No, the thing that put her on edge was the arrogance of the tail, the way he or she purposefully allowed their footfalls to be heard, yet not seen. This served to heighten her stress with every passing moment until she reached the steps of the quadruplex, fully piqued with nerves. The simple task of locating her keys was impacted by the amped up tension, making her fumble, which was unacceptable. Flicking her gaze backward again, she jumped when a leaf scuttled across the concrete, adding a dash of irritation to the mix.

The first inklings of fall had begun to tease out some color in the trees, all set to transform into the glory of hues signifying a Georgian autumn. August had quickly spun into September without giving Summer much time to contemplate the impending season change when ordinarily watching for nature's shifts gave her great pleasure.

The clinic had been blessed with a recent influx of

patients, increasing so much that Summer had needed to hire part time help. And while the increase in business thrilled her entrepreneurial side, she actively worried about how she would maintain the same level of treatment she prided herself on providing with the number of new clients that had been gained.

All the more reason why being followed now was so jarring. Summer had honestly thought everyone had moved on by this point and there would be no more interest in her—an acupuncture and medical herbalist with a small community-style clinic, intent on simply living her new life. Yet here she stood, hands trembling against the wrought iron after the hasty climb up the stairs, all ready to escape the fresh, unwanted attention.

"Summer Halley."

The voice—definitely male—sounded in the air at the last moment, right as the key was poised to unlock, purposefully allowing her to think she might actually get away unscathed. Disbelief flared, causing her to freeze.

It was clear this person presumed they were in full control of the situation, and they probably were because Summer had foolishly assumed this wouldn't happen again. Her assumption left her unguarded, thus unable to escape the inevitable.

"Who's asking?"

She delayed turning to face him before realizing how unwise and pointless that was too. If he hadn't let her get inside the building without confrontation, he certainly wasn't going to allow her a way out of identifying herself. Besides, he said her name without question, obviously aware he had accosted the right person.

But when she turned, getting a visual of who stood

behind her unnervingly close only served to ramp up her anxiety. This man was menacingly tall and broad shouldered. He wore his dark brown hair cut close, slightly longer on the top with shorter sides nearly clipped to the scalp. Eyes, a slightly lighter tone of brown, never left her face as she took her visual sweep of him.

If she were in the correct mindset to acknowledge the flickering awareness, Summer would have noted how attractive her surveillant was, despite the unfortunate quality of being a stalking, threatening menace. But since he was, and she was effectively trapped, that fact slid in and right back out of her mind.

"Invite me in."

"Now why would I do that?"

The mysterious, would-be assailant smoothly slid a hand inside his jacket pocket and produced a badge, causing Summer's overstimulated pulse to hammer at a different octane. "Special agent Liam Reyes. FBI. Invite me in."

Asking a second time was unnecessary, for as soon as she registered him as authority rather than criminal, she knew she was even more sunk. Lips pressing down into a brittle line to keep them from quivering, Summer turned and let her reckoning walk right through the door.

****

What did one offer an FBI agent who held her fate in his hands?

Summer mulled over that dilemma for a whole five seconds before giving up the notion of playing host and proceeded to plop down into the chair across from where he had already helped himself to a seat, calm and confident in the fact that he could wait out her cooperation. He dwarfed the little drop leaf table she had strategically maneuvered into the alcove beside the kitchen. Again, with a significant lack of physical space between them, his size was disconcerting.

But being intimidated into saying something she shouldn't just wasn't an option. The only logical tactic, as far as she was concerned. was talking her way around this as neutrally as possible. She didn't know what he did or did not know. Far better to adopt a guileless look of confusion over why an FBI agent was following her home from work than to inadvertently reveal something of which he might be none the wiser. The problem was his demeanor didn't imply that he thought her innocent.

Through slightly clenched teeth, she addressed him as levelly as she could muster, "What can I do for you, Mr. Reyes?"

A condescending smile played on his lips, promising the answer wouldn't be short or simple. Instead of responding immediately, he withdrew his phone, studying the screen before rattling off the facts. "Summer Halley, thirty-one years old, sole owner and proprietor of Longtime Sun Community Acupuncture, established two years ago next month. Moved to Savannah in 2017 after attending Florida College of Integrative Medicine. Bought this little historic beauty some eight months back."

Blinking, Summer absorbed each nugget of truth he laid out like a subtle blow. Trying to brace for whatever else was to come, she wondered why he felt compelled to recap a timeline of her life's events. Yet, the more he talked, the more shaken she grew—knowledge was power here. And power equaled control.

"One sister, Katelyn Halley. One ex-husband,

Jerrod Metzinger."

Impatient to get down to it, she cut in, "What's your point?"

"Mother, Emily Halley, residing in Daytona Beach, recently retired," he continued as if she had not spoken. "Father, Richard Halley, deceased in 2008."

In response to being ignored, she glared at him before she could stop herself, then worked to reel it back in with a few deep breaths. She did *not* want to discuss her father's car accident or any members of her family or *anything* related to Jerrod.

She also could not afford to offend her company. Summer attempted to smooth out her expression, soften her tension and appear unfazed. The best she probably got was a look of mild annoyance.

"Participated in an environmentalist rally during college, briefly detained in the aftermath…"

A pause, possibly meant to foster embarrassment, of which she had none over that particular incident. "Listed on EarthScapes' payroll for a considerable length of time before, curiously, being wiped clean. At least on the official books, that is."

Hearing him directly reference EarthScapes and make nod to the existence of unofficial business, had Summer digging her nails into the flesh of her palms. Trying to remain quiet at the precise moment he set the phone down and sent her the look of a predator who'd successfully cornered its prey, pushed her limits.

"Now that we've established a mere snippet of the depth of information we have on you, we can more openly discuss my department's intentions."

"I'm not understanding."

"That's because I haven't discussed anything yet.

Trust me, it will become clear enough once I do. You will, hopefully, cooperate without any further push back."

Summer swallowed a knee jerk retort about "pushing back" along with the strong desire to let him know exactly how she felt about his passive aggressive approach. Anger was preferable to fear—at least, for her, it was less debilitating to her wits.

When she instead resumed her hard-won silence, he proceeded with a clearly satisfied air, eliminating the suspense and cutting right to the chase. "We need you to infiltrate Metzinger, establish a point of contact and act as a confidential informant on the FBI's behalf. He's escalated his activities recently, recruiting more associates, and taking on more lucrative jobs. His…merchandise has also increased in places where people know where to find it, the dark web, places where we've been attempting to track."

"What Jerrod does now is not my problem. I don't want to get involved, sorry."

She *almost* denied having any knowledge of what he was talking about, but it was clear, as Mr. Reyes had pointed out, that they had tapped a great well of information already, including her association with EarthScapes. Pretending that she didn't know her ex-husband operated on the other side of the law didn't seem like the best idea anymore.

"Well, Ms. Halley, it is your problem, and you do need to get involved. Or should I say, reinvolved. Because from where we're sitting, we can trace you to accessing several offshore accounts that have been connected to previous employees of his. Most of whom have been apprehended and met with numerous charges, some related, some not, yet none of them would flip on Metzinger."

"So, you're getting desperate?"

He smiled a smile that was all teeth but refused to take the bait. "We're hoping that you'll see things differently and decide to help yourself out while also helping us along the way."

They knew.

The flood of panic was so intense it seized her heart, her stomach, her vision and almost sent her doubling over in the chair. Reeling back against the physical reaction to the implications of what was happening, determination clawed its way through, reinforcing her refusal to not give up. Yet.

Slowly, slowly, the only outward movement Summer allowed herself was a repositioning of the grip on her hands, instead white knuckling them beneath the table as the fight to keep her fear out of sight from Reyes raged. For several blinding moments, her clinic and everything she had worked so hard to create and define as her own, flashed through her mind as she imagined it all being ripped away and having her dream crushed. Of her going to jail. Of her finally being held accountable for those wrong and stupid choices she had made in the past.

"Trust me, Ms. Halley, it's really not you we want. It's Metzinger. But if you choose not to take part in this, you will deal with the repercussions. Your business license, all your patients, that's not going to keep well if you're convicted and incarcerated."

"You're threatening me," she managed to choke out.

"Indeed. But a better way to look at this is that I'm merely outlining what will happen if you decide to take the path you want to take instead of making the smart choice and work with us."

Strangely, his arrogance helped lessen the distress. She was able to straighten her spine once more. No, she wouldn't make this easy and she wouldn't meekly turn over and give up her life. Not without a fight.

"Work with you. As if I'm some sort of contractor."

"Confidential informant."

"Whatever. As your *confidential informant*, how exactly am I supposed to convince Jerrod to interact with me again, let alone trust me? Our divorce wasn't exactly…amicable."

"How you go about mending bridges is the least of our concerns, just as long as you get it done effectively without blowing your cover. I guess we can hope you're a better actress than the performance you tried putting on for me." Leaning forward, he dropped his voice to a mock whisper. "By the way, your face is very expressive and far, far from innocent."

Summer caught the undertone, the ever so suggestive undercurrent and was appalled at herself when a dash of heat bloomed low in her stomach. Even when he leaned back again to resume a safer distance, the ache took several moments to dissipate.

Regardless of the context of the comment, what he just said was true—she was far from innocent, and he'd scented her guilt like a bloodhound.

Truly mortified over all the angles of this horrific situation, she resolutely clamped her mouth shut, refusing to give away any more than she was already sharing and ignored the way her body had briefly responded to him.

After a few more moments of being studied, he

continued. "Once you infiltrate Metzinger and regain his confidence, we expect you to communicate consistently and with transparency, even on what might seem like only the most mundane of details you're reporting. And rest assured, we will know if you stray. We will know everything you do."

He let that statement linger into the heavy silence, no doubt understanding how effectively he was getting what he wanted out of her.

"So, Ms. Halley, do we have a deal?"

Chapter Two

The clinic's reclining chairs remained full for the better half of the three-hour treatment window.

Summer usually loved Fridays, using the shorter appointment time to balance any administrative tasks to end her week on a calmer note. One wonderful thing about running her own business was the ability to define her own schedule.

Today, however, was a trial of misery as she finally ushered the last of her patients out the door, filled an outstanding herbal order before beginning the mundane but painless responsibilities of inventory, bank deposits, and patient record updates.

She could blame it on any number of things but obviously knew the real source of her strife. Long after Mr. Special Agent Reyes left, his presence remained palpable, infiltrating her senses and violating her equilibrium. As if her condo was now tarnished with the guilt that had been the key to their leverage.

All those awful feelings she normally worked hard to keep locked away in their own private section of her head and heart felt permanently exposed and strewn about her home, providing constant torment.

Shoving things to the background wasn't coping with them, but she had come too damn far to dwell on history that couldn't be changed. And when she thought too long about the past that continued to haunt, it inevitably spurred renewed anguish over her angel baby Keira and her sister Katelyn's diagnosis. And the compartment inside of her heart cracked open a little bit wider, but always deep enough to pull her down and suffocate.

Useless, angry tears threatened as she stared at the computer screen; she stubbornly shoved those down too. Now was not the time for crying, it was time for planning.

All the unknown people on this task force appeared to have confidence in her ability to be the puppet on the string. They thought they had her trapped, which was true enough. So that meant she would have to work out her own slice of control if she was going to make it out of this in one piece. And even then, her mission was bound to leave a few more scars.

Not only did she have to pretend to want Jerrod back—there would be no other way to effectively garner his attention—Summer was being forced to give up information that might result in further implicating herself. Even though it had been more than a year since their divorce had been officially filed and she was collectively less aware of Jerrod's recent heists, there was no erasing the prior knowledge she possessed and the previous role she had played. If there was still evidence linked to her...she feared no amount of cooperation would save her from facing federal charges.

A significant piece of her entertained running. She could go stay with her mom in Florida or beg Katelyn and her brother-in-law Gabe to assist with hiding her out. But a bigger, more sensible side of her realized that if the FBI already knew about the many facets of her life, they would know exactly where to look if she fled. And fleeing would still mean giving up her clinic, sacrificing all that mattered in the niche she'd carved out of Savannah.

Absently, Summer's eyes drifted over to the decaled lettering adorning the far wall, the words claiming the namesake of her clinic. Reading the yoga blessing was usually soothing, even if the words carried tiny barbs of despair disguised in the calm it offered. Of its own volition, her hand fluttered to her flat stomach as she breathed in the words of the Longtime Sun, comforting a phantom life that would never be born.

****

Twilight had begun to edge across the cobblestones by the time Summer exited the clinic. Savannah was already buzzing with the promise of an evening full of indulgence and intrigue. The city pulsed with energy, heightened by the increase in pedestrian traffic signifying this hour of an impending weekend night.

She'd left later than usual, unable to harness enough focus to complete what needed to be done in a timely manner, but nonetheless, had gotten accomplished. Once moving beyond a few social groups loitering between destinations, for a bit, it was only her steps audible on the stones which made the swirling rampage of thoughts too loud to be comfortable.

"Ms. Halley."

Not the interruption she was looking for.

Jolting, Summer whipped around at the sound of Agent Reyes' voice floating out through the waning light. She could hear him, yet not see him, making her briefly wonder if she was imagining the whole thing. But since she doubted she'd gone entirely crazy, she had to admit—he was extremely good at remaining undetected.

Had she still been in the game, Summer would consider his skill set to be an excellent asset to Jerrod's crew, despite the irritating personality flaws. But she wasn't and he was upholding the law, not breaking it.

"Agent Reyes."

He materialized out of an alley entrance, one heavily obstructed by creeping jasmine and several oversized dumpsters. "Nice evening for a walk."

"You're not invited."

For a split second, he actually grinned at her, instead of defaulting to one of those annoying, condescending half smirks. "Didn't I already warn you it's best to invite me?"

She opened then closed her mouth, unable to come up with a clever enough response.

With a grumpy, audible exhale, Summer allowed him to fall in step, taking a position slightly behind her left side since certain sections of the sidewalk didn't allow room enough to accommodate two unless you wanted to get real friendly with your companion. She most certainly did not.

For several blocks, neither spoke, which allowed ample time for her nerves to kick in full blast. Again, she was hit with the sensation that he knew exactly which tactic would work best.

Reyes wanted her off balance and unsure of herself—and was obnoxiously successful at accomplishing it. Just when Summer was about to break the silence and demand to know the reason for his second appearance so soon, he surprised her with an attempt at small talk as they approached the next crosswalk. "What year was your building built?"

"1886," she replied icily.

"Convenient to be within walking distance of your clinic. And in a very lucrative slice of Savannah's historic district."

Summer kept her eyes averted as they kept walking. Clearly not small talk. He could insinuate all he wanted; she would confirm nothing. Maybe he was able to access financial records that showed unknown income outside of her business. But she doubted he—or his team—could trace the source to Jerrod, disguised behind EarthScapes, buying her silence after the split. Except EarthScapes was already on their radar.

When she didn't elaborate, he continued. "We need you to make initial contact with Metzinger by tomorrow."

Coming to a dead stop, she whirled on him, mouth gaping. "Tomorrow?"

"That's right. At the latest. If you felt so inclined as to avail yourself to us tonight, that would be even better, but I expressed to the team that you would probably feel more comfortable with tomorrow."

"You thought I would feel more comfortable." She drew out the statement, emphasizing the absurdity of each word. "Since when do you care about my comfort in any of this? And are you the only member of your team I'll have the pleasure of dealing with?"

She got the sense he was holding back a laugh, subsequently making her want to gnash her teeth. Digging deep for self-control, she kept them in a mostly straight line, neither smiling nor snarling. Mostly.

"At the moment, yes, but that's not something you need to worry about either. What you need to be worrying about is how to be convincing when you approach Metzinger, how you're going to play your hand. You probably won't get a do-over, Ms. Halley, so you need to make this first time going in count."

Their walk resumed. She wasn't quite sure how her legs started moving again, only that Reyes had some sort of nonverbal influence over their pace. With the quiet relapsing, Summer rapidly ran through the implications in her head. In reality, she would never be *ready* to approach Jerrod, let alone make that day be tomorrow. She had slammed so many doors closed last year, determined to sever all ties to him and their previous life together.

Yes, he'd had her followed. Yes, he'd been involved in her financial stability, but those seemed like small prices to pay in exchange for the gusts of fresh air she could now breathe deeply in the midst of her new freedom.

And she would be throwing all that away in order to protect that freedom. That was if things actually went well and she was able to convince him she wanted back in. Not to mention staying in long enough to gather the necessary intel. Intel that could make a difference to this investigation. Intel that could help keep her freedom and take down a well-run organization.

Her stomach rolled, threatening to regurgitate her earlier lunch. Traitor did not sit well in her soul, even when dealing with someone such as her ex. "Got any other sage advice for me?"

"Don't try being anything other than yourself. Your value to us lies in your connection to Metzinger and it's that connection you're going to want to exploit. Disingenuous leads to dangerous."

By that time, they had reached her stairs. Summer, assuming he would leave her just as inauspiciously as he had the previous day, twisted her face into another scowl when Reyes continued right up after her. "I take it we're not done yet?"

"Not even close, Ms. Halley."

There it was again; the minute tone shift she concluded she must have imagined yesterday. The one that had caused the undesirable reaction in her blood, despite knowing it was far safer to let the suggestion stay in the imagination category. She would berate herself later.

Giving him her back, Summer unlocked the door with a jerk and led them inside. Depositing her bag on the counter and grabbing some water before circling back around, she didn't anticipate seeing Reyes still standing exactly where she'd left him. He made no move to sit at her table like yesterday, choosing instead to hover near the threshold as though not wanting to address whatever else he was here to say. Which made little sense, for that authoritative air to falter a bit.

"We need to discuss several key points before you go out tomorrow," he eventually said.

"Such as?"

"First, the FBI will install a tracking app on your phone along with the audio streaming feed. This way we can communicate, verbally or otherwise, with you as well as hear everything you're saying to Metzinger when it's turned on."

"Okay…can't you just do that now? You're here and I don't feel very inclined to let you keep my phone until tomorrow."

"I could but I won't be going far in the interim so I doubt it will make much of a difference."

"What do you mean?"

For a moment, his brief uncertainty reappeared, causing a rise in Summer's nerves. What topic could possibly be worse than anything that he'd already thrown at her? Well, things could always get worse—she knew that better than most. But still…

A barely audible sigh slid out as he rubbed a hand along the back of his neck. Then quickly dropped it and resumed his usual, impenetrable expression. "I will be monitoring the situation from here on out, keeping the team apprised of your whereabouts moving forward into tomorrow."

In her limited experience with cops, Summer had already grown weary of all the evasive talk. "And that means what, exactly?"

"I'll be here, during the intervals, when you're out completing your tasks."

"You mean you want to stay here? In my house? While I stay at Jerrod's? Absolutely not."

"Unfortunately, Ms. Halley—"

"No," Summer jumped in. "First off, I refuse to live with that man again. Refuse. And second, you have no right to move in just to make your job easier while I'm gone."

"Not to point out the obvious, but you're not exactly in a position to be negotiating with us. And it's not about making my job easier, by the way, it's about ensuring a well-run operation. It's about success…with expediency." He cocked his head. "Would you prefer it if we all come in and set up the entire surveillance team in your guest room?"

Summer gulped some water to temper the fire in her mouth before her anger spun too far out of control, and she said something she regretted. "If those are my only two choices, I pick option A."

He nodded in a way that indicated he never doubted otherwise. "You won't even know I'm here while you're away."

Summer sincerely doubted that but decided to move on to her next point instead of continuing a fruitless attempt to bargain with this man. Because that was like bargaining with the steel walls of the bureau, and with her fate.

"To circle back around to what you said earlier about authenticity, Jerrod is far less likely to believe I want to get back together if I proposed moving right back in with him in one fell swoop. I'm not even sure he's going to go for it like it stands anyway, but he'll definitely know something's up if I just drop all my stuff at his doorstep and announce my burning desire to immediately play house."

"Why is that?"

"Because he knows me well enough to know I wouldn't forgive and forget like that. He would think I'd want time to test things out, like a trial run, if we were ever to do this in real life."

"This is real life, Ms. Halley."

"Not to me, it's not," she snapped. "I'm trying to protect my real life, not ruin it. So, I have to make this believable. And Jerrod would not believe that I'd blindly accept a reconciliation. Talk about disingenuous."

"That bad of a breakup, huh?"

She didn't dignify that with a response. Instead, she pivoted to start pacing before deciding, screw it, and moved over to pluck a bottle of wine out the wooden rack situated along the wall near to the alcove.

Pointedly, Summer poured one solitary glass before

returning to the living room with lips pursed against the edge as she watched him survey the surroundings.

She saw what he did, the original hardwood floors, which had been refinished somewhere down the line, but not so perfectly done as to diminish the character accentuated by the lived-in blips and blemishes.

The space was modestly sized with a combination living and dining area that connected to the petite, L-shaped kitchen nook, which featured additional modernization. A small window above the sink showcased a shady courtyard. Her favorite thing about the entire place was the woodburning fireplace in the larger of the two bedrooms.

Overall, the townhouse had a unique blend of old and new southern style and suited her well. And although she'd lived there less than a year, Summer had been determined to make the space feel comfortable and entirely her own, adding touches of things she loved, either through bold colors or accents of oriental flare.

"You have an affinity for interior design."

"I didn't think you were one for compliments, but thanks. I tend to pick out what suits my tastes and the space, which is rarely anything boring or basic."

"Have you ever traveled there? China? Indonesia? Seen any of the places you clearly love so much?"

"I can't tell if you're being sincere or mocking me again."

Something flickered briefly in his eyes then was just as quickly gone. Maybe he had rightfully thought better of asking more personal questions. Or ones that didn't serve official purposes.

When he didn't comment further, Summer said, "At least I can rest easy knowing my choice of décor meets your approval. Oh wait, that would be what *you'll* be doing here, while I'm sheltering in the lion's den. Not exactly restful."

This time Reyes did let loose a succinct chuckle. "Noted, Ms. Halley."

More softly, she added, "No, I've never been to Asia, although that's a dream for someday."

A brief nod came as acknowledgment of the statement, followed by all business restored as Reyes motioned her over to the table and proceeded to walk through the app installation and how to use the technology.

His exit afterward was a momentous relief.

Once she was alone again, Summer refilled her wine and headed outside to the bistro table tucked beneath the sweet gums, unable to remain within the mounting restriction of four walls. The courtyard was a shared one but, thankfully, no other neighbors were out tonight.

Greedily sucking the night air into her lungs as though she'd been long deprived, she absorbed the energy shift of the darkness, the living pulse inciting an immediate change to the rhythm of her system.

When she was younger, Summer had been less able to anticipate these mood shifts, often riding on the restless energy with no clear path or outlet. It was during one of those reckless head spaces when she'd first met Jerrod, crossing paths during a night out, bar hopping down along Bay Street. Thriving on the rush and loving Savannah's nightlife after having recently graduated and moved in with Katelyn, their meeting had been a collision of similar spirit. Or so it had seemed at the time.

Her sister had been out with her that night, encouraging their hook up, as though the instant connection between them was something special, something rare.

Later on, she began to see ways that Jerrod indulged that wild side, being a fuel to the flame burning inside her, begging for a channel. Maybe exploit was a more accurate term, she thought now. He knew which buttons could be pushed to exploit her impulsive streak, which is probably how she'd lost sight of right from wrong when she had first begun helping out on jobs.

Then again, if it hadn't been for Katelyn's cancer diagnosis, Summer never would have needed to do so in the first place. The timing of her sister becoming sick had come crashing down on all of them. But it became all the more pivotal while Summer was in the midst of completing final clinicals for her master's degree when the doctors discovered the first tumor on Katelyn's ovary.

Early enough, they'd thought, and after the surgery, Katelyn enjoyed a blissful period of remission.

It was during that excessive night out, after she'd stupidly come to believe that Katelyn would stay okay, when her sister broke the news of a second tumor. But by then, they'd widened their sources of support, even with Mom situated in Florida. Or so she'd thought.

Katelyn was engaged to Gabe and Summer had found Jerrod. And when it became apparent that Katelyn was drowning in financial problems, Summer moved out of her place, in with Jerrod and eventually became groomed to accept the more lucrative ways he made his money.

It had been a systematic process, for she hadn't known what he really did until she was in too deep to back out unscathed. For a long time, Summer had believed Jerrod ran EarthScapes and all those on the payroll made a sole living providing lawn and landscape services. He'd assimilated her into the illegal side of the company by degrees—an odd request here, a simple need there—before she realized how ensnared she'd become.

Thinking about impulse control issues inadvertently brought her around to Reyes. He appeared to be another male who exacerbated those questionable personality traits, most specifically her verbal filter. A piece of her was appalled to think she'd spoken to an FBI agent quite so flippantly, while another, darker part wanted to relive the baited aggravation just so she could set him straight all over again.

Bottom line, Summer might not like his arrogant attitude and maddeningly impenetrable facial expressions, but she was being forced to cooperate with him while being used as a means to an end. Therefore, she needed to treat him in kind. By doing what they asked, by betraying Jerrod, she would, in turn, be staying true to her post-divorce goal—keep her clinic and everything that she cared about firmly in her possession.

Anxiety over this insurmountable task surged strong as the wind kicked up, fluttering in the drying leaves and swelling the air with a tempting temperature reprieve as Summer drowned in all that could be lost if she failed.

Chapter Three

Because she knew Reyes had an obligation to follow her, Summer purposefully rose earlier than usual. Dressing for a run in the dusky dark of first light, she then detoured over to Longtime Sun to ensure that the sharps containers had been picked up as scheduled.

If that was merely an excuse to further disrupt his morning, so be it. After confirming her containers were taken care of, she set out on an extended run, winding down streets at random, always aware that Reyes maintained a steady presence behind her. When she rounded Forsyth Park, sweat trailing her spine despite the early hour, she went with her gut and spontaneously changed directions toward Abercorn Street.

For a few delicious moments, Summer couldn't sense anyone behind her, and she inwardly gloated over the idea that she had succeeded in losing him. Even though that glee only lasted several minutes before she perceived company again, the pettiness was well worth it. Eventually, however, she got tired of her one-sided cat and mouse game and returned to the townhouse for a long shower and a game plan.

When she emerged, hair dripping and wrapped in only a towel, she nearly jumped a foot to find the object of her ire reclined on the couch. Grasping the towel against her chest, Summer sent him a death stare. "Excuse me, what the *hell*?"

In response, he merely held up a key, letting it dangle along with a smirk, before dropping it back inside his jacket pocket. "In the event that you're indisposed or simply unable to let me in, this is a necessary safeguard."

He said it so damn reasonably, as if he hadn't just broken into her apartment. For a second time Summer found herself opening then closing her mouth, unable to produce a comeback that wouldn't result in making things worse.

Her state of undress was also distressing, so, without another word, she retreated back to her room in order to find something suitable to wear for seducing an ex-husband. If the idea made her stomach quivery and her pulse pound, she would just have to push past it. There was no other choice.

She tried to block the part of her mind actively fuming at Reyes while the other part was growing sick over the prospect ahead of her. If only she could fixate on making a selection of something form fitting but with enough coverage for comfort. Which resulted in chastising thoughts because there would be no comfort in this mission whether her skin was exposed or not.

Reappearing after giving her light brown hair, recently chopped into a collarbone skimming lob, a tousle dry and a few spritzes of texturizing spray— thankfully she could pull off the wash-and-wear look pretty well, having been gifted with natural waves and decent volume—Summer sailed across the living room and deliberately avoided eye contact.

Only once she'd retrieved her phone from the charger did she join him near—not next to—the couch. A few beats passed before he prompted, "So this is the part where you tell me how you plan to get into

Metzinger's."

There were the nerves again, fluttering madly. She wished she'd had time to give herself an acupuncture treatment but that clearly wasn't going to happen at this point. Next day in the clinic, she resolved she would give herself a stress relief session and chill out for a full thirty.

In lieu of a needle, she applied pressure to the web of skin between thumb and forefinger and drew in a full round of breath before answering. "At the moment, the plan is to go to Jerrod's house and ask if we can talk."

Apparently assuming she had more to say, an expectant look crossed his face before his eyes narrowed. "You mean to tell me that that's all you've got? Ask to talk to the guy? Ms. Halley—"

She held up a hand, "Listen, you all enlisted *my* help, implying that you feel I can be an asset of some sort. Correct?"

When his brow furrow deepened, she continued, "Exactly. You think I can do this. So, if you do, then you need to trust me when I say this has to be nuanced. If I go blasting in there all demanding and being extra about stuff, I can guarantee you, the game will be up faster than the time it took for you to break into my house."

He seemed to mull that over before adopting another inaccessible expression. "Fair enough," he offered. "You determine the best way you think to make an initial…impression we'll call it. If, for some reason what you do doesn't work, then you agree to allow me to dictate every word you say and every move you make, if you get my drift."

She definitely got it. Appalled, Summer vehemently shook her head, "Absolutely off the table."

"Thought you wouldn't like that one. So, make it

count Ms. Halley, so we don't have to resort to drastic measures."

Swallowing hard, she nodded instead of speaking since the idea of seducing Jerrod had formed a jagged lump in her throat.

He returned her nod with a brief one of his own. "Okay then. You ready?"

****

On a good day, when she was in the right headspace and the weather was cooperative, Summer could, in theory, walk to her ex-husband's new digs.

At the time when he had helped fund her own move, she'd been unaware of his intention to stay quite so close by. During the separation, their shared apartment lease was mutually terminated, neither party interested in occupying the space after things deteriorated.

The only real assurance there was that she was fairly certain, after everything had gone down, that he had fully gotten over her in the process. His ability to rebound would have been much easier, given her evolved understanding of his narcissistic qualities.

Love didn't make Jerrod tick. Money, manipulation, control—that was his language. Summer could only wish now that she hadn't been so late on the uptake to have figured it all out.

Maybe then.... No, she resolutely banished the thought. Maybe then nothing. Because maybe then would have meant that she wouldn't have gotten those few, precious moments with Keira growing inside of her. Even if it meant the consequential torture and turmoil inflicted from the demise of their marriage.

But she didn't want to think about her angel baby now. That path wouldn't help her tap into the strength she needed to execute the task at hand, nor would it help reinforce the armor she needed to wear the more she interacted with Reyes.

And unfortunately, the task at hand had arrived far faster than she realized.

Summer slowed her steps, having already reached the correct row of housing in the midst of being too caught up in a past that couldn't be altered. Twice she stopped before reluctantly locating his number because while she knew abstractly which was his, Summer had never come here, never investigated. It was vital to her mental health that she firmly shut the door on their collaboration once it ended.

Yet here she stood, in the face of her failure, with the knowledge of how dire everything was resting on this crucial moment. Summer made herself push the ring button—then took in the view while he made her wait.

There was a distinctly upscale vibe to the exterior, one that ran toward deep southern wealth. It wasn't just the building's location in the northern historic district or the prestige of nearby Chippewa Square. The exclusivity in the Baroque-style design details rubbed her the wrong way. Like it clashed with the authenticity of embracing its historical roots.

She tried not to squirm beneath the scrutiny of the doorbell camera, but it couldn't be helped. Finally, after a purposeful amount of time had lapsed, Jerrod eased open the door. Resting a shoulder against the frame, he eyed her up and down, not bothering to temper the predatory, yet questioning, look that crossed his face.

For a moment, her tongue felt like it had turned to sandpaper, incapable of producing articulate speech. Then, slowly, she worked up a tentative smile—one she willed to look a little lost, a little hopeful.

"Summer. So sorry to keep you waiting," he drawled lazily. "Quite surprising to see you slink back over here. Didn't think I would ever see that happen again, but, hey, I guess when times get tough, people get desperate."

Swallowing her pride in one harsh lump, Summer processed that Jerrod assumed she was here for money. A distinct part of her acknowledged the logic of that assumption, while the rest of her warred against the shame she felt from that idea being not so farfetched.

Was it so much of a stretch for him to think that was why she had come here? All the distance she'd gained, all the growth away from another life that fed off negativity had been reduced, diminished by that one implied statement. "Actually, I was just hoping we could talk."

Another speculative expression flashed across his face as those cool, blue eyes openly perused the length of her body. "Talk." He repeated the word like it was mentioning something taboo or, conversely, inconsequential.

But without further debate, he moved aside and let her in, shocking her with how simple that first step had been. And the instincts that kept screaming out to turn away couldn't be acknowledged, not when she'd just accomplished gaining her audience.

If Summer balked at how close he followed behind her, she tamped that down too and instead focused on observing the interior of his residence. By comparison to her place's mix of modern and historical charm, Jerrod's tri-level townhouse boasted an entire array of sleek upgrades and slick finishes. If one didn't know they were in Savannah, nothing about the inside of this home indicated they were in the south. To Summer, it completely ruined the charm of owning space in a historic building in the first place. But this was no longer her problem. No one was interested in whether or not she appreciated the style of the apartment.

Turning slightly, she aimed an appraising look back toward the reason why she was here, which was easier without his eyes trained directly on her. He looked the same, yet not. Physically, Jerrod's physique and everything she had once known by heart hadn't changed. At just slightly taller than her own five foot, six inches, he didn't let his lack of height impress upon anyone that he was one to be messed with. Hard, cut muscles showed beneath his sleeves and his sandy blond hair was cut ruthlessly short, shorn even shorter than Reyes' tight style. And while both men might possess an arrogant streak, Jerrod's arrogance encompassed a much wider—and far more menacing—span.

An image of Reyes, alone in her apartment, floated through her mind before she could squash it. Thinking about that man at this present moment would only be another detriment.

Firmly refocusing on Jerrod, Summer noted that there was also a subtle difference in the way he moved inside this place, a distinct shift in the air as he sauntered throughout, as though he could allow all those dark parts, the manipulative facets of himself, to take full reign here. He didn't need to hide anything within the privacy of his own home, and it caused a shiver to vibrate down her spine watching what was usually kept more camouflaged.

One could argue that he had a right to be arrogant.

He'd never been caught before; no friend or enemy had been able to cinch such a deal in order to effectively take him down. Not like her. Apparently, she had been an easy pick, a prime candidate for being used for something like this.

Suppressing the unpleasant flutters, Summer checked her phone as casually as she could to reconfirm that the FBI app was active and listening. They were waiting. Waiting on the other line to determine that she was doing her job. Well, step one was done—get inside.

But Summer knew step two was going to be infinitely harder.

Chapter Four

She gestured toward the opulent kitchen, the view out the large window revealing a lush expanse of green space. "This is elaborate, even for you."

They settled on the leather sofa, Jerrod lounging back with ease as though she was just an old friend, stopping over to catch up. For her, it was impossible to assume such a casual stance, but she at least tried keeping the stiffness out of her posture. "Not exactly keeping a low profile."

"Now, would that be worry for me I hear?" He sent her a familiar, cheeky smile. "Don't be concerned, Summer, I've got nothing to hide."

Long ago, that smile would have charmed her. But she knew he used it as ruthlessly as any other resource so long as it got him what—or who—he wanted. "Not worrying, just observing. Has work been, um, steady?"

Again the smile, except this time accentuated by a slightly harder glint, reminding her that this is where things got sticky. She considered just how much she should ask, just how far she should push on this first day. Not being privy to the FBI's timetable didn't help but Summer sincerely doubted they were a patient bunch.

For a second, he hesitated, lifting up out of the reclined pose, the movement sending a sliver of apprehension through her system. It was the only indication that her question struck a chord. "You could say that." he shifted, sliding back to a slouch and waving a significant hand at all the wealth she'd just spoken of, like the house should speak for itself.

Just a blip on his radar—she hoped—but Summer also acknowledged that she would have to tread more carefully.

"So, are you going to tell me what else is on your mind? Because I don't think you only came by to get an eyeful of how I'm living now. What do you want, Summer?"

The words were there, hovering behind her teeth like some poisonous thing that could neither be swallowed nor spat out. Left inside, they would fester and rot, yet if released…she would be bound to a fate somehow worse than her previous life.

But there was no choice, she had to spit. "I was hoping…I was thinking we could work on things between us. You know, like try it out slowly. We have so much history together."

"That we do."

"It's weird now, being on my own."

Again, an ever so slight tightening in his pose, the only subtle sign that he was piqued. Or intrigued. "You never did like sleeping alone."

There was little point in confirming what they both knew and every reason to pretend she believed he could care.

When had he gotten so good at that? A chameleon, donning a fresh skin whenever it pleased him. Or a snake, poised to strike as necessary but never rushing because he understood how lethal he could be. If he wanted.

It appeared to be all about choice.

And just like that, the conversation turned to easier topics. The question wasn't whether or not the move was intentional—it most certainly was. Summer never doubted that Jerrod knew he had taken full control of rerouting the focus of their talk. It was the why that had her perplexed. Why he was letting her off the hook for the time being, allowing her to get away without producing a more concrete reason for showing up unannounced.

Abruptly, his phone interrupted a half-hearted recount of one of his earlier conquests. Whoever it was, Jerrod immediately ceased his attention on her and rose to speak to the caller out of ear shot.

Which meant no tidbits of information to be gained.

Summer waited, uncomfortable at best, crawling out of her skin at worst. She tried concentrating on the lesser, telling herself it wasn't that bad, everything was fine.

The minutes were only a handful, but they dragged on in her mind until he finally reappeared. Jerrod addressed her so, so coolly as though they hadn't just been reliving different times. "A project requires my immediate attention."

Unconsciously, she had risen when he'd come back into the room, certainly as he intended for her to do, but also as a sign that her body was begging for a way out of this stress. But this was his turf, he would always need to feel as if he had the upper hand.

"Good to see you, Summer. I look forward to our next…attempt. If there is one."

Abandoning any attempt to offer something resembling reassurance, she simply nodded before making a hasty retreat to the front entrance. Already back on the phone, Jerrod unceremoniously shut the door behind her as soon as her feet touched the brick.

Now outside, unrestricted and alone, Summer fought the urge to yank out her own phone and shut down the app. Certain people were avidly listening, so intently she was sure, they could hear her pounding heart and elevated breathing straight through the speaker.

Realizing how close she was hovering toward tipping over the panic line, Summer stopped, unclenched her hands and drew in some deep breaths. It could have sounded a bit like growling, the angry way her breath blew in and out of her mouth, but at least she was *trying* to center herself.

The desire to turn and run burned strong in her blood. Fantasizing about an island, a small village—a glorified fucking hut—where she could treat her patients in peace, without interference…she came close to muttering a mirthless laugh over the fantasy.

Now look who was the one being ridiculous. But at the moment, she felt like she'd earned the right to be. The problem with indulging that kind of mentality, however, was that it wouldn't do any good for helping her get out of this mess, only make things harder.

She began walking, one foot in front of the other, trying to keep rational thoughts flowing before she did anything rash. By the time she crossed through several city squares, she felt entirely justified in shutting her phone completely off. But before she could hit the side button to lock the screen, she found herself staring at a missed text sent from an unknown number.

Assuming it was Jerrod, she almost swiped the notification to the side, planning to read it later when she could properly deal with him again. Then her thumb slipped, opening the message instead of dismissing it.

—I see you—

Her heart pulsed, thrumming to a roar.

Jerrod had never admitted to stalking her before, it had simply been deduced. And she had never confronted him over it either, wanting only to move forward and wipe the slate clean. Was he reviving old ways in unfortunate timing to the FBI's arrangement? And if he was, why would he...taunt her with it?

Smashing down the lock button, Summer powered off the phone and broke into a jog.

Once she reached the haven of her own steps, former justification took on a destructive edge as Reyes yanked open the door before she had a chance to make contact with the handle. "Ms. Halley, get in here. Now." The demand was bellowed through a steel-clenched jaw, in an obviously failed attempt to stifle his profound irritation.

Summer, fed up with men and the entire fucking day, rolled her eyes and breezed right past him with forced bravado as though it was exactly what she intended to do anyway. If the brush of her body against his bicep amplified the crackling energy, she chose to tell herself the charge was from all the hostility floating around.

"Did I or did I not make myself clear when I said that we would be monitoring your *every* move from here on out?"

"Crystal."

"Then tell me what the hell you were thinking turning off your phone? We lost your location just outside of Metzinger's property."

Weary, down to her core, her false assertiveness

withered beneath the combative nature that took over whenever she talked to Reyes. "Look, I'm sorry. I just needed a private moment."

Forcing eyes to meet his, unsure of how vulnerable it might make her, some of what she was feeling showed through because the aggressive snarl curving his mouth softened. Unconsciously, her gaze traveled down to that mouth, held for several beats before she realized just how intently he was watching her watch him. Yanking her stare away to a far safer section of the living room, Summer desperately wished he would leave now that she was back home but knew that was a lofty desire.

She would need to be briefed, provide a thorough recap even though what she really wanted to do was suggest he simply recall what he'd heard on their spy app. Talking it all through again was too daunting. Yet, instead of doing what she feared, he gave a stoic nod before tucking away his tablet, signaling dismissal.

"Good job today, you got inside and didn't expose anything. But we're just getting started."

Whether or not he meant it to sound ominous, the statement echoed within the walls of her refuge long after he showed himself out, the hollow promise her only remaining companion.

Chapter Five

In a way that felt oddly too normal, Summer navigated the gamut of issues her patients threw at her the following day with a scraped together amount of grace.

If she could do nothing else to calm the white noise in her mind, at least she could be a healer, a listener, to the people who sought her out for that comfort and relief. Fertility issues, migraines, addiction, depression. Those were problems she knew how to tackle, harnessing the body's healing energy and signaling the correct meridians.

If her heart split a bit during a consultation with a new client as she described the pain she'd endured during a recent miscarriage, Summer concealed the chasm creeping open inside of her chest by offering a tangible treatment plan. Objective goals plus productive action equaled her opportunities to atone. Despite that intention, she fought to avert her eyes from the Longtime Sun wall whenever she moved between rooms.

Once the last of her patients were awakened from their acu-naps, Summer began her closing routine. Fiddling with sheets—a job that was usually taken on by Ayana—she reminded herself that this was why she had originally hired the art design student. Alleviating simple tasks from her plate would help her be more effective in advocating for more patients. But right now, the mundane provided stability.

Once the linens had been stripped from the recliners, Summer turned off the salt lamps and the endless loop of ocean waves floating up through the floor speakers. In wonderful silence, she made it back up to the front desk to address any final notes and check emails. Then, retrieving her phone, Summer reread the earlier text from her sister, the one she had been neglecting to answer. Apparently, Katelyn had another oncology appointment.

It wasn't that she didn't want to be kept in the loop—far from it—but her brain had reached maximum capacity since Reyes had entered the playing field and one more piece of bad news might send her into overload.

It was a poor excuse, even to tell herself. Summer would be supportive and call Katelyn or Gabe later to find out how it went, no matter how stressed she felt. It was not okay to leave them hanging.

As she stared at the screen, a sudden heightening in her senses alerted her that someone had entered the room, even with one hundred percent certainty that she'd flipped the deadbolt thirty minutes ago. Stiffening, she lost her grip on the phone, letting it tumble onto the desk with a significant *thunk*.

"Didn't mean to scare you."

His voice sent goosebumps racing down her skin, a split-second thrill. Then she looked up. Reyes, towering inside the waiting area that now felt too tight, too suffocating, held up his palms in mock surrender. He shouldn't look so towering—or intimidating. She could handle herself. And him.

But seeing him here, in *her* place, that felt immune from the current nightmare controlling her life, crushed the calm she'd worked so hard to establish in her little healing cocoon. It was naïve to think her clinic couldn't or wouldn't be touched by his reach, but it still felt like a major violation.

What Summer wanted to say and what actually came out were at active war within her head. "To what do I owe the honor of your presence?"

Something in her delivery must not have been convincing. Instead of resuming their verbal sparring match, he did a slow, methodical turn, stopping to read the quote christening the entryway—much to her chagrin. "May the long time sun shine upon you. All love surround you. And the pure light within you. Guide your way on."

The words tumbled into the quiet, heavy as bricks, whether or not he was cognizant of the weight they carried. He obviously couldn't know. The FBI couldn't access medical records…or assign meaning to a phrase she held dear.

Summer cast her gaze away when she felt her game face faltered. And then, suddenly, he was close, too close, a witness to the discomfort etching itself onto her features. Her grief, when triggered, was like a thumbprint, unique to her and disguised to few.

"Ms. Halley," he said softly in a voice transformed into something almost kind, "Would you rather we talk in a while? After you've finished here and have gotten settled at home?"

Unnerved by his abrupt change in demeanor—at least the verbal combat was something she had come to anticipate—she stared back at him, feeling at a loss. Now he was acting so understanding, like he could possibly have a clue as to the source of her affliction.

Sighing out a fractured breath, she broke the trance by running a hand through her hair and tugging a piece behind her ear. "No, let's get this over with. What do you need, Agent Reyes?"

A slight restriction held his posture before he straightened away from her desk, as if it had just become apparent that their close proximity wasn't helping matters. "I—we—," he amended, "Need you to make contact with Metzinger by the end of the day today."

"Why today? I just successfully spent yesterday afternoon with him."

"I—we—feel it's important you don't let too much time pass between communication attempts in order to make the infiltration efficient. You know, capitalize on the headway."

"You all don't feel like I'm operating at a quick enough pace? Too bad. That criticism's unwarranted, considering this thing just got started. Since all of yesterday."

Right on cue, his irritating brand of cockiness returned. "Ms. Halley, be advised, *again*, who you're dealing with here. The bureau doesn't play kindly with pushback and insubordination."

This was what she told herself she could deal with— the full of himself agent who had become her personal babysitter. Not someone who felt sorry for her, even if he had no idea why she'd become upset, aside from the obvious stress he and his department were inflicting upon her.

"Insubordination? Really? Don't gaslight me. I was blackmailed, not hired."

"Which worked out well since we actually have something to blackmail you for." He arched a brow, driving home the point.

Summer picked up her stylus, tapped the tip, pretending to consider declining the request. "Fine. Done. I'll text him shortly. Now please leave."

"If it bothers you that much, me coming to your clinic, I can keep our meetings strictly to your house."

"And why would you care if it bothers me? When have my feelings become a concern of yours?"

"Since I have been tasked with ensuring your cooperation and the effective execution of your role in this operation."

"No. You've been tasked with that since last week and not one iota of your *effective execution* has cared one bit about what does and does not bother me about it."

"There's where you're wrong. Unfortunately. That being said," he continued smoothly, halting any attempt she might make to cut in and ask what exactly he meant. "I'll touch base with you later on tonight to review any texts you exchange with Metzinger."

Without another pointed word, Reyes turned quickly on his heel and let himself out, calling back without turning around that she should lock up behind him.

"Ugh, fuck!" Summer aired her frustration into the empty room. Infuriating fucking man.

But as irritating as Reyes was, what was wrong with *her*? Many people had walked through those doors, had stopped to read those words. Why did *his* reading of them cause such a visceral loss of composure?

If she had the inclination to analyze the situation—no, scratch that. Not only was she not inclined, she truly could not afford to divert any extra energy toward triggers that were only temporary.

Temporary. This whole, terrible thing was temporary, and she'd figure out a way to deal with it. Picking up her phone again, Summer drafted a new text to Jerrod before closing it down once more as the taunting one liner from yesterday etched itself across her memory.

Bothered that it bothered her enough to consider sharing the creepy *I see you* text with Reyes, she ultimately decided against it. They probably wouldn't care that Jerrod had resumed stalking her during this process if it meant that he cared enough to let her get close to him again.

She'd neither responded nor deleted it and rereading those three words now caused trepidation to lance through her. They had been down this road before, this wasn't new. But the boldness of it was.

Telling herself she wasn't procrastinating, she instead sent a message to Katelyn, letting her know she'd check in later. Then she called her mom.

"Hey, what are you up to?" Emily answered after a few rings, sounding slightly out of breath.

"Not much, just closing down the clinic for the day. If this isn't a good time, you can call me later. I'll be home."

"Are you sure? You sound antsy."

Antsy. Another understatement for feeling like her life was careening out of control. A significant metallic sound echoed over the line. "Mom, seriously, it's okay. You're in the middle of something…"

"Well, I decided to try this SUP class out here at Silver Beach. We're about to head out to the water."

Summer couldn't help but smile at this news. It was bolstering to hear that her mom was trying something new. For an exceedingly long time after her dad had died, Emily so rarely stepped outside of her comfort zone. Channeling all her energy onto Summer and Katelyn, she went through many years as a shell of her former self. Richard and Emily had been so close, loving the outdoors together, all before the crash permanently shattered certain aspects of her mom's personality.

Yet here she was, after all this time, attempting a stand-up paddleboard class. Pride filled her heart and Summer tried tapping into Emily's bravery. "Then I'll let you go adventuring... just want to tell you though, Jerrod and I are trying to work things out," she got it out as fast as she could manage. And before her mom could interject, Summer quickly added, "Please go enjoy your class, it sounds exciting and challenging. We can talk later."

After a long beat, Emily spoke softly, the worry leaking through, "I love you, Summer Leigh. Call you after."

The disappointment in speaking his name aloud to her mother was not unexpected yet still rolled waves of despair inside her stomach. Suddenly not caring if Reyes was waiting on her or that she had yet to hit send on Jerrod's unfinished thread, Summer cracked open a new pack of needles, tapped them into the stress points and closed her eyes for ten blissful minutes.

****

—Hey, how's your day going?—

—Lucrative. What do u want, Summer?—

—To talk. To work things out—

—We talked yesterday. And I don't think you're interested—

—I told you I am—

Skye Mueller

*—Must have been other than your words. If you do
mean it, come by tomorrow night—*
—I do mean it. I'll see you then—

Chapter Six

"You were apparently less convincing than we thought."

Summer refrained from rolling her eyes at the comment. Pointing out her failure was so unnecessary, unless you were an FBI agent whose job it was to micromanage criminals into compliance. Then it was probably perfectly necessary.

She and Reyes were out in the courtyard—a much easier setting instead of congregating within confining interiors. It came as no surprise that he had been there waiting for her when she had arrived home that evening, but no more welcomed.

The abbreviated acu-treatment had helped smooth out the edges so maybe that was why it hadn't really fazed her that he'd utilized his key. But the fact that it didn't set her teeth squarely into his ass, she couldn't be sure of what that said about her headspace.

Surprising them both, Summer even offered up a second glass this time when she opened a bottle of wine, and he surprised them further by accepting. To an outsider, their meeting looked quite intimate. A couple sitting under the stars on a clear, crisp fall night. Enjoying some wine and one another's company.

Except if someone were to peer a bit closer and make out the dark circles slicing under Summer's eyes or the tension pulling at her mouth. Or see the way her phone sat between them on the table like a piece of incriminating evidence, the situation took on a more sinister edge. As they both stared at the typed conversation exchanged just before she'd left Longtime Sun, her phone suddenly illuminated with an incoming message.

"Do you want to answer your sister?"

For some reason, the question threw her, and Summer whipped her gaze up to his face. She knew he knew about her family—and in great, lengthy disturbing detail. It had been one of the more damning points brought out during their first meeting so there was no escaping this. They knew her, they knew her family. All the more reason she had no choice but to comply.

"I told her I'd call her later."

"Would this constitute as later? If so, I can wait if it's something important." His lips quirked into a brief smile. "Don't worry Ms. Halley, I'm not going anywhere."

Of that she was certain. Biting down a retort about the FBI's intolerance of her productivity, Summer retreated to the farthest corner of the courtyard since Reyes insisted on being so obliging. And even beneath the shroud of the sweet gums, she was aware that he could probably still hear her. Could certainly still see her and most likely her discomfort. She hit the call button anyway and Katelyn answered after the first ring. "Hey, what's been up with you? You're not usually so out of pocket on a clinic day."

"Yeah, I know, sorry. Things got a little...complicated this afternoon," she offered, determined to keep the guilt at bay. Katelyn knew her schedule, it had rarely deviated since Longtime Sun's inception. Stability. Responsibility. All the adjectives Summer had been driven to establish the moment the ink had dried on the divorce filing.

"Isn't the new girl helping out? What's her name? Ayana?"

"Yes, and yes, she is. It's just…" Again, she trailed off. If Summer had fed the lie to her mom, she would have to do the same with Katelyn. It was only a matter of time before she found out anyway. Better to have it come straight from the source. "Me and Jerrod. We—"

"Did you really just say that asshole's name? Summer, I can't believe I'm hearing—"

"I know, I get it. But listen, Katelyn, it's just that we're talking again. I don't know if things are going to work out but that's where it's at as of now and I wanted you to know."

Her sister fell silent for several, brutal seconds before exhaling a tired sounding breath, reminding Summer that she needed to focus on Katelyn's health, not her own disaster of a situation. "Tell me what the doctor said, please."

"Well, it's what we figured. He confirmed that the meds didn't shrink the tumor, but it has prevented it from progressing. There are a couple of options."

Summer felt her stomach tighten. Options for treatment almost always meant picking the best of the worst, especially if the medications hadn't worked.

She listened, cringing by degrees, as Katelyn talked through the radiation procedure and an optional ablation process. Injections had wrecked her the first time around, so how would this second tumor react if they took a similar approach?

It was on the tip of her tongue to ask how Gabe was

Skye Mueller

handling everything, including the financials, but she couldn't get the question out before her sister abruptly wrapped up and ended the call. Probably due in part to the Jerrod confession but it had been unavoidable.

The ensuing silence was as loud as a scream releasing into the inky night when there was no more talking and only the knowledge that Reyes was waiting for her mere feet away. Closing her eyes for a moment, she absorbed the deflation along with the punch of helplessness before digging deep for composure. Knowing he had heard most, if not all, of the sensitive details, Summer unceremoniously landed back down into the bistro chair and took the offense by scowling at Reyes, daring him to say something. If he did, she really wouldn't know how to deflect or deny the insight he'd just gained from being nearby.

Apparently, he chose to take the high road. "Shall we continue then?"

Relief mixed with some other confusing emotion as Summer processed that he wasn't asking about the call.

And if he had questioned differently, inquiring about the doctor or the obvious reaction she'd given, what would be the benefit or harm of him knowing Katelyn had cancer? So that he might understand her previous motives just a little clearer? Did she care whether or not he truly understood the reality of the situation, the reasons why she'd chosen to knowingly and repeatedly break the law?

This perplexing notion that some small part of her *had* wanted him to ask, *had* wanted him to hear the real driving force behind her deception did not sit comfortably inside.

"You okay?"

Summer exhaled. "Earlier, I had to lie to my mom, just now to my sister. *Okay* is kind of relative at this point."

"You lied for the greater good."

"Ha. That should be your motto—oh, wait—isn't that already FBI mentality? As long as it's for the greater good, it doesn't matter who gets disrespected or screwed over along the way."

A long beat passed, causing a heaviness to cloud the deep brown of his eyes as he leaned back in the chair. Then it cleared, replaced by a hard, impenetrable coating. "That certainly is their way of thinking. One I'm all too familiar with since my father was one of those who got screwed along the way."

Despite knowing it was better to stay in her lane, Summer asked anyway, "What happened?"

Another moment passed before Reyes responded. And when he did, it was with a voice gone cold, drained of all emotion. One that only focused on the brutal truth of recalling the events. "He was a line of duty kind of officer, always finding himself taking the more dangerous calls, being in the midst of the more life-threatening situations. He liked it, I guess, the thrill that can come with it. Back then, I was a beat cop too." He smiled thinly. "So I understood a bit of that thrill, that rush, especially when the outcome is favorable. He always tended to think he'd end up on the right side of things, even if the odds tipped less than favorable.

"Anyway, we were both working, although on separate calls like usual, the night he got caught up in an FBI case. A kidnapping. My father wouldn't leave, even though it was no longer his jurisdiction. And when things took a turn, the situation got heated, they let my dad

49

continue the pursuit. Let him engage the fucker who'd taken the kids. He ended up getting killed for it and it was okay because it wasn't one of theirs. Through his involvement—or probable error—the FBI ended up apprehending the suspect right after the exchange. After they let my dad be taken down."

Watching him look devoid of feeling, as concealed to the world as if wearing an armored mask, Summer absorbed the idea that he too understood the anguish of losing a parent and it was like a shot in the blood. The fact that he had experienced the same life altering tragedy as her, Summer willed back the thickness swelling sharply in her throat.

Concluding something else, she murmured, "So you joined them after that."

In a way that should have been frightening, Reyes reared forward, eyes skewering hers with such severity, Summer couldn't fight against the instinct to shrink back a little. "You're damn right. I know this foe, I can study it, keep it close."

Neither spoke for several minutes after that. Left to contemplate many things in the time lapse, the one she circled back around to was that maybe, by exposing this piece of himself, by allowing this personal, painful moment to be known to her, Reyes was purposefully opening the way for her to reciprocate.

Unfortunately for him, he was about to be sorely disappointed.

With questionable dignity, Summer unearthed her phone again, pulling up Jerrod's texts as though the last ten minutes had never happened. "So, your take on this is that he doesn't believe me, and my take is that he's testing me—a sign that means he's not sure. His instincts could be wrong. Or not, but he doesn't *not* believe me so it's like a test."

Apparently willing to pretend right along with her, Reyes' eyes lit with a measured level of humor, the hard shell receding. "As convoluted as that came out, I get what you're saying. It's not over and he's intrigued enough to do a trial run. Good."

"Yeah. Good."

"Tell me about a client today."

"Excuse me?"

"Not who they are or anything, just some anonymous person who you saw today. How did you help them?"

Summer considered the question. She didn't know Reyes, especially not in terms of his belief system or views on alternative medicine. In her eyes, acupuncture and herbs shouldn't be considered alternative, but she had encountered many people who felt the need to tell her differently. If he didn't trust the approach, nothing she shared would change his mind on the topic. People were decidedly narrow in their ways and she'd met many. What was one more?

"The last patient I treated is set to be induced in two days if she doesn't naturally go into labor before then. Because modern medicine doesn't trust human bodies to do what they are made to do, they want to intervene with the process on their timetable. If she's not in labor yet, it means the baby's not ready to come, but that makes her overdue, which is a medical no-no. Anyway," Summer continued with a wave of her hand, "I gave her a therapeutic treatment to help reduce swelling in her feet and stimulate contractions. Hopefully, I hear from her in the next twelve or so hours and she'll be well on her way without additional medical intervention."

She pictured Brielle, so nervous and excited and incredibly overwhelmed with the prospect of childbirth. There had been a time when Summer had considered pursuing becoming a birth doula and advocating for expectant mothers. That was before the night with Jerrod and Cameron changed everything for her.

"You sound confident in that outcome," Reyes said.

"The body has the power to heal itself, I just help free the stagnation and channel it, bringing out what should be intuitively occurring on its own. If you held out your tongue right now, I could decern the effectiveness of your digestion, whether or not you have a blood deficiency and if there are any imbalances in your liver energy."

Faltering, Summer stared down into her glass, contemplating why he wanted her to open up. Weren't things weird enough that she was forced to associate with him? Inexplicable or not, his interest seemed genuine, and she detected no level of judgement or disbelief.

When she felt her determination to remain unaffected waver, replaying in her head what he'd shared about his father, exposing an undeniable thread of commonality, the easier it would be to just lower the wall a little more.

Abruptly, she scooted her chair back. "So…I guess I'll see you tomorrow night."

She couldn't believe things between them could get any more awkward, but she was wrong. At her sudden dismissal, he actually appeared caught off guard. Was she supposed to pretend to be hospitable to him, keep him around after discussing theories? How many times had she asked him to leave? Every time they were together by her count.

But this was different, his reaction to the end, as though her words were taken as some sort of rejection. And she *hated* the hollow feeling that began to creep in when it was only her left at the table.

So much so that, despite knowing how it would serve to worsen the emptiness, Summer couldn't stop herself from going inside, retrieving the slim folder she kept tucked away in her bedside table. It was slim because it had only accumulated four months' worth of mementos but each item in it was a treasure.

Picking up the first ultrasound picture as though it were made of fragile glass, Summer cradled it in her hands and stared down at Keira.

Her baby's outline, her shape, at sixteen weeks along was fuzzy and distorted. And so very tiny. But no matter how small, the life that had been blossoming inside her had ignited an enduring flame of restitution. Her mouth opened, the agony escaping on a strangled gasp. She pressed Keira's image to her cheeks, to her eyes, and eventually to her stomach, wishing with every molecule that there would have been some way to keep her safe in there until she had been ready to come into the world.

Summer had determined her own choices, her own path. And because of what she'd chosen to do, the wrongs she'd chosen to commit, she had failed to protect her unborn child.

Chapter Seven

Summer waited until night fully cloaked the sky before she descended the stairs, leaving Reyes lounging on the couch with who knew what to occupy him besides this endeavor they were sending her on. Procrastination wouldn't help matters but that evening energy added a little extra oomph to make the impending event slightly less offensive, teasing out the night creature in her.

Per her keeper's suggestion to appear more available, her body was wrapped in a snug tunic-length sweater with black leggings and combat boots. Despite the thinness of the fabric, the tight material kept her warm against the chill in the air.

This time Jerrod did not keep her waiting; instead, he met her at the door with an amber colored ale, already poured into a glass. The full body look he raked her with, however, lingered far longer than the last time. Ripe with promise—or threat—Summer felt the intent straight and clear to her heart. She clenched her fists in order to battle back the repulsion while her face held steady and smooth.

"Summer." He stretched her name, drawing it out for the duration of the visual sweep.

"Jerrod. Thanks," she replied lightly, forcing herself to take the offered glass.

With a bit of flourish, he stepped back, sweeping open an entrance as if gallantry was second nature before leading them out to the courtyard. Whether or not it was for her benefit, Summer was grateful they would be outdoors though it felt weird to consider if her former spouse thought about her preferences or needs any longer. It was a notion she figured would never come up—but here she was, drinking a preferred beer with the man whom she'd once sworn she was done with.

And he knew her so well.

Settling in across from him, she put a slight arch in her back, allowing the body-hugging dress to work to her advantage. Moving, stretching, positioning herself in such a way that appeared effortless, while betraying none of the intention or necessity behind it.

"Productive day?"

Her question dripped of feigned interest, and she knew she'd succeeded when, like a charm, he became more fixated on the presentation of her subtle curves rather than by the fact that through asking, she was setting up to dig for info.

Eventually bringing his visual perusal up to her face, he replied, "Very. We have a new…focus for the time being."

"Do tell."

At the slight narrowing of his brows, Summer forced more curve into her hip. The humiliating move worked, and the crease on his face settled once more. "I've got a few associates scoping out some automotive possibilities."

"Hmmm…sounds different for you, definitely."

"You could say that. Or you could say this is a long time coming, given the amount of time I've dedicated to our organization's success. You would say I'm an opportunistic sort of man, right?"

Unsure of his angle, Summer offered a tentative smile, a slow nod of agreement.

"Then you can understand why this would be a natural progression. But even a few of my most loyal hires don't think we should stretch into too much unknown territory. That we should stick with what we know, stick with what works. And you know what I say to that?"

"What's that?"

"That uncharted territory, when researched properly, is what brings our employees their security. What feeds their kids and keeps their side pieces dripping in designer. If I didn't aim high, their asses will inevitably resort back to scraping the bottom with petty theft bullshit and all that luxury they're accustomed to goes back to being just a dream. Just like you."

There it was: the taunt, the bait. He sent her a smile, knowing she would have a hard time not rising to the occasion of being called materialistic or selfish. Or reacting to his attempt at playing the martyr.

Gulping at her beer, Summer battled to keep her tongue in check. The catastrophic repercussions of failing to be convincing had been made all the more clear when she left Reyes earlier.

He had emphasized the requirement, telling her several times that if she couldn't make progress tonight, if she were unable to procure a viable piece of information, the FBI might see it time to disregard the arrangement. An arrangement, he felt necessary to remind her again, was to her benefit as well. Benefit—as in being preferable to a felony conviction.

Even if she felt like they were wanting the impossible out of her, she couldn't fail at this. Jerrod *had* to believe she was sincere. And *she* had to balance her questions while obtaining useful pieces of intel.

So, her tongue held against the steel of her will and when he realized she wasn't going to give him the expected retort, he arched a brow at her response. "You're right, Jerrod. We've all grown used to wanting our dreams to stay our reality."

A piece of her felt smothered beneath the burden of lies, the weight of deception but there was no going back.

"Speaking of, what's the clinic like these days? Still going strong?"

"Thankfully yes. I even had to hire part time help because I can't spend as much time tethered to the front desk."

"I wouldn't expect any less. You set your mind to it, then you're going to make it happen. Still don't get why you did the acupuncture route though."

She absorbed the compliment and criticism in stride. His approval was irrelevant now. But she had to feign that she cared. "I know you thought I should go conventional nursing from the beginning, but it's been quite a while since that was an avenue I even marginally entertained pursuing. You know where my passion's at."

"That I do, yes."

With significance, he let his usual expression drop for a few beats, revealing desire and darkness. That look could drown females and males alike, especially those who didn't know him or those who didn't care about the source of the darkness.

Fighting a tremor, Summer quickly rerouted the direction, "If you start targeting cars, how much harder is it to liquidate the earnings?"

That did the trick. The barrier went back up and his

attention snapped away from her body. "Again, I have to wonder, do you worry that much about me, Summer? Or is it that you worry there might be something that could put you in a difficult position."

If her mouth dropped open, just a little, at odds with the level of concentration it took to play it cool, he didn't comment.

Instead, without explanation, Jerrod disappeared into the house before returning with another round of drinks, not caring whether or not it was wanted or requested. Smoothly refilling her glass, he allowed his body to purposefully press against hers, the position she'd been using to keep him divided now coming back to bite her, literally in the ass.

Summer felt his erection pulsing hotly against her hip, nudging at her butt. Recoiling internally, she remained steadfast and held still as stone while he jutted his cock toward her center. Then he withdrew himself, resuming the space across the table as though it never occurred.

But while his expression might have remained inscrutably blank, Summer knew he was gauging her response. Bathed beneath the dim glow of strung Edison bulbs, she felt exposed. Guilty. And horribly aware of her inability to fake things.

"In answer to your question about liquidity, we are fortunate to have acquired a few new employees who can assist us with the process. You left big shoes to fill but I'm relatively confident we are, at least, stretching our toes forward and finding our way."

"On the EarthScapes side? Or both?"

"Both. It would seem their abilities are varied, so I can use them in multiple ways, but always, always for my benefit."

"Naturally. So, nothing came out of Darren's, ah, apprehension?"

"That fucker?" He shrugged, like the guy hadn't been on his payroll for several years, hustling and pulling jobs with ruthless efficiency. "He knew what he signed up for and he kept his head down and mouth shut with the cops. I guess he got the picture that even locked up, I still have my ways."

Ice slid through her veins at the harsh reality of Jerrod's lack of humanity. She shivered, knowing how unpredictable he could become when not being made to abide by the rules. Then his camera app sounded, drawing out a deeper shiver as it sent illuminating light out from his phone. She hadn't realized how deep the dark had settled.

"It's Cameron." As if she wasn't there, Jerrod scooped up his phone and strode back into the house.

Cast into the void, the relief stemming from his exit so intense, Summer expelled her revulsion on one gusty exhale which melded in with the draft instantaneously. Then the truth in all of that blackness hit hard. She had not seen Cameron since the day she lost the baby.

And if he was here now, interrupting on a night she was sure Jerrod would have made clear not to be disturbed, something must have gone wrong on a job. That lack of humanity might be making another appearance.

Her head and heart engaged in a vicious volley. If he let Cameron in to deal with the problem, if she was forced to interact with him because of all the bad luck plaguing her, there was a chance she could walk away with something solid for Reyes. Or Jerrod could keep whatever the problem was under wraps, because even though Cameron was one of his most trusted, *she* was the one he wasn't sure about. But if she was forced to interact with him now, Summer was terrified of what could be dredged up from the depths.

Her internal battle culminated with another unwise decision.

With an unnecessary sweep of the yard—there was no one here but her—she felt her feet begin to twitch. There was no one here, not yet. There was no authority to stop her, only the felons she didn't want to align with. She *was* the FBI's eyes and ears, and she was about to close both of them to sound reason.

Impulse thrust out her hand, pulling the last dregs of her beer into her mouth and then snatching up her clutch, Summer abandoned all semblance of cover and bolted for the back gate.

****

With every step, logic kept screaming to turn back, to fix the mess. But with every step, the mess kept spreading, much like the distance she was gaining. She'd just ruined everything, destroying the rare opportunity all because she couldn't cope with the past. Even knowing it, knowing how fucked up she was, she still fled, unable to face Cameron or Jerrod. Or herself.

Her phone kept vibrating, and she knew without looking that it was Reyes, alerted to the fact that she was on the move earlier than projected, based on the plan. The plan that she had just shot to shit. Again, she thought about running, escaping somewhere. And again, she knew it would be pointless.

The only direction she could run now was back home before Jerrod—or worse—came looking for her.

As Summer rounded her street, left with nothing but the last resort, on cue, Reyes yanked open her front door before she had a chance to make it to the top of the stairs. "Ms. Halley," he greeted through gritted teeth, jutting a finger toward her living room, "In. Now."

As if she didn't know what he was about to say. As if she needed an invitation to get out of sight. Alcohol alleviated the effort of keeping her filter in check and why had she thought she couldn't speak her mind to him from the beginning?

She stomped up the last few steps and jutted her chin toward him, riding on a wave of defiance. "Screw this entire thing and you with it. I don't need to put myself through this, I don't need—Let go!"

Appalled, she pulled back when he reached a hand down to cup her elbow. Except cupping would imply that the grip didn't feel like forged steel. No, this was no gentle effort or subtle guidance intended to send her where he wanted her to go.

Caught between his unrelenting hold and glare, without a word, he shut the door with a sharp rap and escorted her over to her own damn couch. Jerking free as soon as the vise grip lessened, Summer stalked back and forth a moment, running a hand through her hair and fuming at Special Agent Liam Reyes' audacity.

He remained silent, all while watching her with unwavering focus until she eventually ceased with some of that testy jerking and turned back around to face in his general direction. "Tread very, very lightly, Ms. Halley," he suggested with velvety softness. "For you to put yourself through this, you need to play nice. Unless of course you're hoping to try out your luck in the lovely legal system. Maybe you think that pretty face of yours will make things go easier, lighten the severity of the outcome if you bat those beautiful blue eyes just right." His voice dropped a few more degrees, like hushed, coated steel, barely restrained. "If I were you, I wouldn't test it."

Gaping, her lips then peeled back into a disgusted snarl. How dare he think she'd try to whore her way out of things? Use her looks to make things go her way? Except isn't that exactly what he'd threatened she might have to resort to with Jerrod anyway? Isn't that what she'd just used to her advantage tonight?

Self-loathing roiled in her stomach. "As offensive as the suggestion is, maybe it would be better to take my chances with the courts than to subject myself to the very people who helped ruin my life in the first place."

It wasn't really true because there was no one to blame but herself for that, but she certainly wasn't able to say that out loud. Battling the nausea, she struggled to keep it wiped clean from her face because the few defenses she possessed revolved around the effort to appear unaffected by what was happening.

Reyes studied her for a long moment, too long. "What happened?"

She squirmed beneath the reasonable tone, the imploring look. She took a quick mental inventory before responding, having forgotten the actual useful piece of information Jerrod had dropped in the midst of being swallowed up by her own aversion. The question Reyes just posed could be taken as a personal inquiry and she did not want to go there.

Grabbing the news like a lifeline, she countered, "I found out he's hitting cars now; I'm just not sure in what capacity—or how. There, now you have something valuable you can give to the higher ups."

The ensuing quiet was immense. In defense, she grew more indignant. "What, you're going to tell me that's not good enough? Not helpful enough?"

"You said it first. Now I don't have to."

"Then I guess it's not good enough."

"Who is Cameron?"

"One of Jerrod's associates, a very trusted one who's been with the organization for years."

His eyes flared at the word organization, as if using the phrase to describe a theft ring was truly offensive. But he only asked, "And you left before he arrived?"

"Yes."

"Because?"

"Because I knew Jerrod wouldn't say anything else in front of him while I was there," she lied hastily. "Even if Jerrod believes I'm willing to try again, Cameron wouldn't buy it. At least not at this point. So, he wouldn't put sensitive information out there like that or show that he's willing to expose them to the likes of me."

"I see."

He didn't see anything, but as long as he trusted the excuse, the presumed reason for her departure, she wasn't about to cast any light on her shadowed heart. "Can we be done for tonight?"

"If that's what you want."

Her gaze whipped up to his face, assessing, gauging. The tone shifted, like he was baiting her, using those unnerving undercurrents that wove between them to ignite her emotions and let the full force of what she was feeling come to life. The way he sometimes watched her, the way he occasionally let suggestion color his voice.

He'd said she was beautiful and was looking at her

now as if that were true.

Staring at the rich brown of his eyes, she thought she read invitation there but had no idea if she could trust it, no idea if it wasn't bound to some other motivation.

Was it her imagination or was this an opening to exploit? On her own terms? Like he knew what she just might do in this moment, in this headspace, given the opportunity. It just as quickly flickered away again as her stare became more direct. She was left straining against better judgement and self-control with the desire to make the opportunity reappear.

Summer purposefully inched closer, peering up into his face, one that had adopted a mask ironically similar to Jerrod's. Except his lacked an inhumane bent. And while he might be just as intent on concealing his own emotions as her ex, Reyes appeared to be having a harder time succeeding as she eliminated the space between them.

She watched, deliciously thrilled, when his pupils expanded. She could hear his breathing grow slightly uneven, see the pulse throb in his throat, as she invaded his senses. Did he want her to stop? Did he regret where he'd pushed her?

A flash of self-deprecating clarity slammed into Summer along with the repercussions of what she was about to do. In every way that Jerrod had destroyed pieces of her, Agent Reyes was well on his way to leaving his own dose of damage. Although not necessarily because he wanted to. He was doing his job. Like Jerrod had been.

She really needed to stop comparing the two.

"You've gotten this far," he said. "Are you going to see it through?" Reacting to her hesitation, he said it like a dare before gripping her around the waist and pulling her fully against him, sealing the decision.

It was she who moved next, to mark that anticipated joining of mouths. Instantly ignited, she felt relentless and demanding all because he felt so achingly hot against her lips. The scorching heat plunged deep down into the cold place she carried inside her chest. Into the chasm she didn't care to acknowledge. The corrosive place she didn't want to accept, even as it craved this type of solace.

Lost to the urgency, when she felt herself floating at the shimmering edge of losing all remaining shreds of common sense, Summer slowly, dimly became aware that his lips and tongue weren't actually moving. Only allowing her to take everything she needed from him but not willing to offer reciprocation.

Shame was a violent douse of water so cold, her chest now felt brittle and fractured. Grabbing ahold of her pride, she shoved him away. Both watched the other, wary and apprehensive, as if each had stumbled onto something wild and untamed. And unexpected.

The sound of his phone ringing served to highlight her embarrassment. He remained motionless for a moment, apparently unwilling to soften the blow of mortification. Then, intentionally keeping his eyes on her face, he slid his thumb across the screen. "Reyes."

The curt greeting he usually answered with sounded a bit more on edge, but Summer refused to read anything into it. He'd just *stood* there, goading her into a lip lock and then proceeded to not be an active participant.

No, that wasn't entirely accurate either. She'd been the one to take on the challenge and manipulate things when she had no business messing up their already convoluted relationship in the first place. Even if the desire she'd seen on his face had been real, even if it had only held on for the briefest of seconds before the end result became a disaster.

With no attempt to mitigate, Summer slipped away when his back turned, assuming he knew how to show himself out by now. But he made no move to leave, only exchanging several terse words with the caller before stalking back over to her, eyes blazing.

Awkwardly, she shifted beneath his scrutiny. "What?"

He sighed, just a little, as though he resented what was to come. Then the mask was in back in place, tightening all the little nuances of emotion into a cold, blank stare. "Never assume you have power over me. Never assume that you are the one in charge."

Embarrassed, hurt, she wanted to speak, to deny, but found no words.

When she failed to follow up, his face hardened further. "Exactly. You don't know what rare opportunity you seem intent to fuck up—nor what it will truly cost you. Keep your head in the game, Halley."

His coldness burned, blasting fresh ice over the already frozen pieces in her chest, the ones he'd temporarily thawed during her moments of insanity.

Thinking about that breath-stealing heat had her breaking eye contact. Summer looked away and nodded, silently begging him to take the hint and just leave already. He'd taken enough from her tonight.

The door slammed sharply as he let himself out, giving her what she wished for with all that remained being ugly threats and nasty, unrequited desires.

Blinking rapidly against angry tears, she brushed at

her face, refusing to release the things that stirred within. As if by keeping them contained, it could fix the multiple ways she kept on betraying her own conscience.

Chapter Eight

The silence hit her first, followed by the realization that it was no longer dark. Blinking slowly, Summer registered the morning light with a profound level of resignation. It was Monday. There were no treatments scheduled on Monday. She had no reason to be up, other than her inability to tamp down the barrage of swirling thoughts assaulting her mind.

Last night's escapades had been magnified by her own poor behavior—before, during, and after. Squeezing her eyes back shut, she relived the harrowing details over again, and much to her chagrin, the decision to kiss her FBI surveillant.

Reyes probably hadn't wasted an ounce of energy afterwards, perhaps beyond having a little laugh at her expense. But she feared the inevitable paradigm shift would make things harder, at least for her. Yet he hadn't seemed all that amused yesterday, not even offering her an escape via their usual routes.

He'd acted just as pissed off, which was ridiculous considering his accountability leading up to the kiss. She wallowed a bit longer, engulfed in the familiar sting of guilt, the newfound pulse of regret, before shoving the covers aside like she could shove those trappings away as well. Beating herself up wasn't going to change anything. She was tired of battling against everything that couldn't be done differently.

On a more positive spin, he should at least have the decency to stay out of sight today. No work and no Jerrod communication meant no need to see Special Agent Liam Reyes. She took her time completing her morning routine, even spent a few minutes practicing mindful breathing to settle her system.

With a significant amount of peace restored, Summer scrolled through work emails before heading out to the kitchen to receive a cold slap of reality. Mortified, she saw that she had been very wrong. He hadn't stayed away after all. Had not only *not* stayed away but was, at present moment, cooking breakfast on her stove.

One side wanted to release the rage. Another desperately needed coffee before attempting any human contact. She hovered in the doorway, torn between caffeine and the former, at that moment undetected, before deciding to try and slink past him.

She got as far as the cabinet, poised to reach for a mug before he gave up the charade. "Good morning, Ms. Halley. Mugs are already out by the coffee maker."

She'd been a fool to think he wouldn't sense her. She ground out a terse "thanks" before proceeding to swipe a mug off the counter and fill it to the brim before the pot had time to finish brewing. Sipping it straight black and scalding hot, she could concede that he knew how to brew good coffee and still hate the fact that he was here.

Silently watching him stir eggs in a pan, she noted he was clean about things. No shells or splatter. Just two plates, each with a slice of toast, waiting for the rest of it.

When the eggs were finished, with equally matched

quiet, Reyes efficiently assembled the remaining portion of their breakfast. Summer nearly asked why he had come back, why he felt compelled to cook, but held her tongue until they were seated at the table with the food sending fresh steam up into the air.

She could have resisted, refusing to join him, but instead followed the scent mainly because she was starving. She could berate him after she ate. A few bites in, she was again forced to acknowledge his competence in the kitchen even though her anger simmered.

Eventually, he appeared to discern that her temper, while still brewing, had evened out well enough to attempt conversation. "Now that you've recharged a bit, I wanted to check again if you were able to recall anything else Metzinger said or did last night that we need to know about."

So, this wasn't an apologetic, ass kissing kind of breakfast. Upset with herself over feeling disappointed with his apparent lack of remorse, she replied with a concise, "Nope."

At her refusal to elaborate, he tried another tactic. "I'm curious about how you ended up with a person like Metzinger in the first place."

"Probably just like how everyone else meets someone," she offered evasively, polishing off the last of her eggs. Food had worked its magic toward easing the worst grip of her anger but that didn't mean she had to just roll over. When he shot her a look, Summer sighed and set down the fork. "Fine. We met at a bar, shortly after I moved here."

"From Florida?"

"Yes."

"Okay, so besides meeting in a bar, what about him

appealed to you?" He asked in such a way that made the notion of being involved with someone like Jerrod sound inconceivable. Sure, she felt that way now, but four years ago, thriving on a different kind of emotional high, his draw had been irresistible.

"There was a lot of chemistry at first. He let his intentions be known pretty fast and it intrigued me. After years of dealing with the immaturity of other males, commitment phobias and all that shit, he was the first guy I'd met who actually didn't seem repulsed by the idea of a committed relationship. Anyway," she continued, "We were pretty quickly inseparable; I guess the rest is history. Past tense."

"He doted on you, and you fell for it."

"Well, that's one way to put it if you want to be a smartass."

This earned her one of his rare, genuine smiles. With a shake of his head, he resumed eating and proceeded to clear his plate before speaking again. "Are you going to tell me what had you so freaked out last night?"

"No."

"Ms. Halley."

As if the placating tone would entice her to spill it. She stared at him mutely, silently daring him to repeat the question.

Instead, he continued on with the interview, as if she had actually answered. "Has Metzinger never hit cars before? You reported that little nugget like it was gold."

"Not since I've known him but that doesn't mean much, I guess. He rarely shared about the time before I came into the picture, which should have been a much bigger red flag. But hindsight and all that."

It was yet one more point of contention with the

former version of herself.

She'd had those blinders on for too long and hadn't questioned Jerrod's nonanswers and avoidance of certain topics—not until it had been far too late to get away in one piece. There was probably plenty of stuff that had gone down over the course of their relationship that she hadn't understood or been made aware of its scope. She'd let it happen and when she was reminded of these failures, the result was brittle, bitter self-reproach.

"Then I suppose that is useful information. Anything else jump out at you? Notice anything inside the apartment?"

"No and no. Sorry."

"That's fine for now. Next attempt, we need you to find out where and when if you can."

"A hit, you mean?"

"Yes. The fastest way this can be over is if we witness Metzinger himself committing a crime. He excels at not getting his literal hands dirty, hence why he's been able to continue doing what he does for so long."

"You say that with a little envy."

"Not envy, although admittedly some admiration. I can admire his intelligence, his finesse and still want to take him down. It's the stupid ones who fall fast. Guys like Metzinger make us work, keep us up at night with the challenge. Anyway, if you can draw out a location, something solid, that would help seal this up quicker."

"I'll do what I can."

"Good. Nice to hear you're back to being cooperative again."

When she bared her teeth at him, he only smiled mildly. "Why don't you take some time for yourself today? Believe me, you're going to need it. Take the break."

"And I won't have to worry about anyone following me?"

"That depends."

"On?"

"On what you plan on doing. Keep it clean and maybe you'll have nothing to worry about."

Summer refrained from rolling her eyes at the noncommittal response before moving to help clear the dishes, giving her time to mull over what he'd said.

On one point, Reyes was absolutely right—she really should prioritize some self-care today, even if it was just for an hour. And if she still harbored delusions that he'd been affected by their kiss, then maybe that hour would work toward eliminating those too.

****

Since Katelyn reported feeling better this week, she easily agreed to Summer's suggestion of a slow flow class. As far as murky motive went, Summer dispelled the idea that she was using her sister as a viable escape route, even if she had never felt the need to justify taking a yoga class before now.

Justification seemed like a new requirement for many aspects of her life.

It took intention and a conscious effort to stop focusing on the overwhelming feelings and invisible threats. After Summer cleaned up all traces of breakfast from the kitchen, scrubbing harder than the surfaces required, the need for a reset had her happily booking two slots at their favored spot.

The anticipation was cut short however, when, with timing that was disturbingly in sync with being enroute to the studio, her phone dinged a notification. Irritation swept through her. Had he not promised to stay away from her today? Sort of promised, with not so many words, but still implied...

Except it wasn't Reyes.

—I know what you did—

The unknown number dissipated her positive outlook. Chilled, despite the comfortably warm afternoon, she studied the number, attempting to decipher if it was Jerrod who had typed in those taunting words. But reciting the number cast no clarity, no light on whether he'd resorted to this kind of harassment.

Neither responding or deleting, she shoved the phone away as soon as she rounded the corner and saw her sister come into view. It always shook her, seeing Katelyn without her long hair. And every time she looked away, her sister held her eyes steady, shaming her worse. But these were thoughts that she couldn't bring herself to say out loud. Either that would make her or Katelyn a less good person and she chose to believe that neither option was accurate.

When she caught herself looking back, sweeping glances into the shadows, she told herself to quit being ridiculous. If the FBI or Jerrod's crew wanted to escort her to yoga, then so be it—she had some zen to capture.

****

The class delivered, creating a positive energy release and easing Summer's concerns about Katelyn's ability to do anything strenuous. When Shavasana ended with an extended meditation, one which was particularly melty, she could *almost* pretend it was just a normal day. Before cancer, before Jerrod. Before the FBI had taken her hostage.

As they wandered out of the studio, naturally veering to the left toward their usual coffee shop, the synchrony between them seemed to have returned by significant degrees. In those before times, she hadn't worried about their harmony, gave no thought to a possible strain in their dynamic together.

"I'm glad you suggested this, I needed the mind chill."

"You doing okay? I mean really. Not just what you tell me on the daily."

"Yes, and I mean it," Katelyn reiterated, "For now, at least, things are maintaining."

Relief flooded her and it was immense. Maintenance was the best-case scenario; Summer didn't know how she would navigate things if the answer was otherwise. The conversation suspended for a time as both sisters ordered, dressed their caffeine to taste, then relocated to the row of metal tables lining the outdoor strip.

"The clinic still running too hot to handle?" Katelyn asked once they were settled.

"Yeah, but I've got a better grip on things. Ayana helps out when she's there and my regulars have become slightly more adjusted to potential wait times for chairs."

"That's great. You've fought for it, that's for sure. Try to enjoy the success."

Summer sent her an appreciative smile before sipping at her latte. Then two men, who were lingering near the entrance, appearing to intently study the posted menu, caught her attention. Possibly other agents on Reyes' team? Had Reyes thought she'd need two keepers?

When one of them turned, lowering onyx shaded glasses and looking directly at her with eyes so searing, her pulse rate catapulted to a gallop. If not agents, then perhaps this was some sick game Jerrod was implementing where he had people following her who were impersonating authority. Like some twisted reminder, coupled with creepy texts, that her hands were just as dirty as they'd always been.

Her mind spun. vacillating back and forth between the culprits and she tried and failed to avert her eyes.

"Maybe you needed this more than I did." Through the paranoia, Katelyn's voice sounded hazy.

"What? Sorry, I—"

"No worries. Was just pointing out how awesome my sister is before I lost you."

"Thanks, I think."

Katelyn rolled her eyes. "You work tirelessly for everything you've got. Just be sure you know how to turn it off every once in a while and truly decompress. That's what I've had to tell myself a lot lately."

The two men disappeared into the coffee shop, snapping the draw and putting her attention back on her sister. Good, let Katelyn think she was just overworked instead of going insane. Then her words sank in a little deeper.

"Something else is going on." Summer delivered it as a statement, not a question.

"Nothing crazy. Jeez, don't go low-key paranoid on me." But then Katelyn stalled, her eyes wavering between her coffee and Summer—and Summer realized, alarm stirring, that wasn't completely true either. "It's just…it's been so hard again with the tumors coming back and Gabe being temporarily laid off last spring."

"Hasn't he been brought back on full time now?"

"He was—as of this month—but it was a longer

stretch of time, more than either of us had planned or saved for in 'a just in case' kind of situation. Money—" she let the word hang with all the weight holding it down, "—has been really tight."

Summer compressed her lips. This was just how it all started long ago, beginning with the first cancer go-around and then, shortly after the second occurrence, when she had begun breaking the law. Katelyn, body compromised with illness and unable to work, admitting that she couldn't pay her medical bills. And Jerrod, sly to her obligation and pain, taking his opportunity to utilize her sharpness, her organizational skills, to his advantage. Summer, not wanting to burden their recently retired mother with assuming responsibility for her sister's debt.

Sitting here now, knuckles white around her cup, she ordered herself to remain calm. If she allowed it, things could continue as they always had. She would help however she could and her sister would never ask where the money came from. Or she could remember all the ways she had redefined her life and hold strongly to those convictions. Hadn't she fought to be able to make this choice? To make the right one?

"I'm sorry things are rough again. Do you...I don't know, do you want to come into the clinic on days when Ayana can't be there?"

A pause, coupled with a subtle look of surprise, crossed her sister's face. "I don't know that I have it in me to work right now," Katelyn said. "But I appreciate the offer."

If there was a dash of unmet expectation in her voice, a hint of disappointment, Summer would have felt the sheer heaviness ten times over. But there was also confusion. If her sister was doing well enough to exercise, why weren't part-time hours an option?

She would do anything for Katelyn, so long as it meant not resuming her old ways. Although they never spoke of it, Summer figured Katelyn assumed Jerrod contributed to the cash flow she'd provided, at least in some capacity—because once divorce was on the table, the money had, obviously, come off it. If her sister were trying to lay another path...they couldn't do this the same way again.

Suddenly waving it all away as if her comments were light as air and carried no burden, Katelyn changed course. "Now tell me what's going on with that worthless ex-husband you're apparently willing to give another chance. I swear to God, Summer, I hope he's not holding something over on you."

That hit a little too close to home, hurtled at her in conjunction with the admission of financial worry. And yes, there certainly was something being held over her head, just inflicted by an entirely different entity.

"It's not like that, Katelyn," she offered stiffly, her smile now stretching painfully across her face as though her skin contained broken glass. "We're just hanging out, trying things again."

"Why?"

Great question.

"I miss him."

The statement sounded tainted, each word bearing venomous claws because no matter how acidic the lies tasted, she had no choice but to maintain the ruse.

Katelyn studied her as though she was seeing her in a new, altered light. Summer absorbed her judgment and disillusion without recourse. After a few heightened moments, she settled back in the chair, coffee in hand. "I don't really believe it's that but you're icing me out on this one."

"I'm not trying to—"

"Sure you are, and I'll let it slide for a little bit and respect your privacy over this recent bout of insanity. But eventually I'm going to start prying if you keep it up. Fair warning."

Forcing her shoulder blades back and down, the positive vibes achieved from class disintegrated to ash, Summer drained the last of her coffee right as she felt her phone vibrating through her yoga bag. Knee-jerk apprehension rushed through her again. She shot a glance sideways to see that Katelyn was on the phone as well, probably talking to Gabe.

Moving quickly, she pulled out her phone, grateful that her sister was distracted. Whatever the text was going to read, she wasn't sure she could fix her face in time.

Summer saw she was right but for a completely different reason. Relief washed over her from seeing her mom's photos from the latest paddle boarding adventure, instead of the communication she was dreading from two separate men. Her features twisted in an entirely different way.

"Wow, hey, what happened?" Already back off the phone and tuned into Summer, Katelyn reacted just the way she feared—she read her like a book.

A kooky little laugh slipped out of its own volition. "Here, check out Mom."

Scrolling through the pictures alongside her sister, the looming possibility of having to contend with Jerrod or Reyes rapidly lessening, Summer tried to enjoy the simplicity of the moment and be grateful about not being interrupted after all.

It was Katelyn's phone that ended up being the mode of delivery that brought their afternoon to an abrupt close. As soon as the message sounded, she snatched it up like she suddenly could not wait to get home. "Gabe's about to pull up, I need to get going."

Confusion had Summer asking, "You didn't drive to the studio?"

"No, Gabe dropped me off."

"I didn't realize he worried about you getting to and from yoga."

"Yeah, well, he's been super protective lately and wanted to make sure I got home before—" Katelyn didn't have time to finish explaining herself as Gabe's Jeep whipped into a parallel spot directly in front of the café.

Impatience radiated as he put down the window, the move unwarranted considering the context. "Summer."

Was it her imagination and compromised feelings that had her perceiving his tone as something other than cordial? "Hey, Gabe. We were just finishing up—"

"Coming, babe," Katelyn interrupted to address her husband herself as she grabbed her coffee and barely gave Summer a look back as she left the table. "So glad we got to hit a class, we should try to go more often."

"Wait, Katelyn—"

But the Jeep's door closed shut before she could finish, leaving Summer standing at the curb and watching as their taillights converged with the rest of traffic.

Chapter Nine

Appointments were steady the following morning, and Summer tackled her clients' ailments with renewed determination. Ayana came in right before noon to start her shift, alleviating the number of trips Summer had to take between the reception and treatment areas.

Regardless of the decrease in steps, the busy afternoon flew by; it was only when she realized that she hadn't eaten since breakfast and Ayana had started to gather up the chair sheets, that those who were finishing their treatments were the last appointments of the day.

"Was Caroline the last scheduled?" Summer asked as she made her way toward the back storage and laundry closet.

As Ayana loaded the washing machine, she murmured in agreement before stopping what she was doing as if something just occurred to her. Turning to face Summer, she shrugged, "Yeah, she was the last, but I kept thinking you were getting a walk-in for the past half hour. Guess it's just somebody who doesn't care about designated parking." Turning back to resume the task, Ayana commented, "Really nice ride though. Thought whoever it was would have been breaking the top of your pay scale."

Summer stopped, staring at the girl's back. The clinic ran on a sliding scale payment policy, with the goal of making treatment more accessible to more people.

And the structure of community treatment, where multiple people could be treated at one time, also helped keep costs down on her end.

Not to pass judgement but in her experience, the wealthier crowd tended to gravitate toward private acupuncture settings. And while she strived to create a very intimate, low-lit space for her community practice, more recently having set up several, strategically placed carved wood dividers, Longtime Sun was far from private. And there was the periodic issue of dealing with people who disregarded the signage out front.

Yet, for other reasons, what Ayana said disturbed her.

Easing back out of the storage nook, Summer went through the motions of waking up her final two nappers, ensuring they were comfortable with the removal of the needles and weren't rushing up anywhere too quickly. Then she darted back over to the laundry corner. "Hey, I'll be right back. Can you just double check on the last two out there, make sure they're good on their way out?"

"Yeah, sure," Ayana looked at her a bit quizzically but didn't ask because Summer was already striding through the treatment room as inconspicuously as she could manage when what she really wanted to do was flat out run.

Slipping out the front door, Summer zeroed in immediately on the car that had caught Ayana's attention. An infinite number of reasons as to why it could be parked here disintegrated down to one, betraying the feigned naiveté along with her cool.

The sleek, silver sedan sat like a harbinger, one sent specifically to warn her that she was about to be forced to make a decision. A decision that would ultimately destroy her resolve to never do this again. A decision she couldn't believe she'd have to choose again—and not even to gain the benefit of helping Katelyn.

As she carefully circled the vehicle, rapidly filling up with dread that its presence in the clinic's minimal section of parking screamed Jerrod's handiwork, her phone vibrated with precise timing. Summer tried to steady her hands beneath the punch of adrenaline and unlocked the screen to read the succession of texts.

—*Hey baby, your services are needed*—

—*I want u to be at the designated spot at 4, C will be there within 7 minutes of your arrival. Deliver him to East house*—

—*Key fob on the front left wheel well. Address to be sent to you from a different number*—

—*Just like old times*—

Summer whipped her head around, rotating back and forth as though controlled by some invisible force, pulled by some transparent string. She was, to an extent, because the force of someone watching her was causing her to unravel. She strained to see any sign of Jerrod's men, scanning along the street that was eerily quiet with only a few people walking by, as if identifying the threat could lessen the impact.

Also registering was the horrible timing of her last two patients currently exiting the clinic. She struggled to situate her face into a hospitable smile before the vise grip of fear became too great to combat. "Enjoy the rest of your day; see you next time."

Her voice sounded false, metallic, and she couldn't bring herself to study the faces of those she'd just treated to determine if they perceived anything amiss. A small reprieve that these clients were relatively new to her practice and didn't seem interested in chatting. That was good, that was fine. Under normal circumstances, she would have tried harder to build on rapport, but these were far from normal conditions.

When she was alone again, Summer pressed her fingers along her eye sockets, wishing to eradicate the texted words from her brain, eliminating them from memory.

Then she opened her eyes to face reality. Rereading the messages provided no new slivers of insight. Neither would denying the car's delivery or existence serve to get her anywhere. But one thing was certainly clear enough—Jerrod was testing her, forcing the issue of loyalty boldly out into the forefront. Because, beyond feeding his own ego and serving his purpose, he didn't give a fuck about reminiscing on old times.

C would be Cameron, who was expecting her to transport him to one of the stash houses—specifically the East house, named for its positioning in relation to Savannah's geographical center. There were several locations marked out around the city where the flow of stolen items moved in and out, each referenced by direction only.

It would definitely be just like old times, in every conceivable way that she wished she could forget. Except this time another entity lingered in the shadows, waiting to pounce. Maybe not on her, but to be caught squarely in Reyes' crosshairs…she wasn't sure she would survive it.

Indecision swamped her, rendering her body momentarily inert as Summer wavered beside the getaway car. *Think, think, think.* The only way she had ever survived in Jerrod's world had been by keeping her common sense and maintaining control over her nerves. Thinking about the exponentially higher stakes— thinking about Reyes—would only make it worse.

And there were only fifteen measly minutes left until four o'clock. Either he had been delayed in contacting her, since Ayana had said the car had been out here for quite some time—or he'd purposefully waited until the last minute to summon her, making her cooperation easier to cinch.

She was inclined to believe the latter.

Kicking into motion, Summer took a step, then another, up the length of the sidewalk adjacent to the parking spaces and back down, fruitlessly brainstorming a solution. Or a way out. And coming up empty. At least the movement allayed the nerves to a level, right up until she checked her phone again. Ten to four. She was officially out of time.

With a shaky inhalation, she swiped up her contacts list to find Reyes' number. The call resulted in being sent straight to voicemail.

So, he was busy hitting the fuck you button while she was trying not to lose her head. Quickly pecking out a text that outlined the briefest gist of the situation, Summer also activated the FBI app just in case he bothered to check in on her. Or anyone else from his team, for that matter, since she was only moments away from breaking the law.

Realization that she had known from the very beginning what she had to do came clear and bright. She dispatched the part of her brain that wanted to dwell on the damage this would cause. Finding the key fob, her senses came alive with fresh jitters as Jerrod's next burner phone sent her the promised address.

The hit location was roughly ten minutes away, cementing the notion that he had waited on purpose, guaranteeing less time for her to baulk if she were indeed reconsidering. Sliding into the car, no longer hesitating, she hastily adjusted the seat position and rearview mirror, and felt herself slide firmly into the present. A cool head, calm under pressure—those things didn't seem to describe who she was anymore, but that's what everyone seemed to want to capitalize on. Those old scraps of herself pieced themselves together in vague resemblance but could never fully replicate the original version.

Whoever had last driven the vehicle was significantly taller, so it hadn't been Jerrod doing the deed. Some other minion then, trying to prove his worth to the leader of the corrupt little operation. Or maybe it was the one who was still staked out, alerting her mastermind ex that she had successfully retrieved the car.

Her conscience reared up, helplessly rebelling against Jerrod's inexorable influence. But that was the reason—to define the boundaries and eliminate her ability to choose.

Entering the address into the maps app, Summer methodically backed out of the parking spot. Anytime she felt her focus start to falter, struggling to channel everything toward executing Jerrod's directives, she reminded herself that lack of success would mean destroying everything. Everything she surmised would be ripped away from her in the end anyway.

It was a weekday, hovering around traditional end-of-day hours, and the traffic was unforgiving. Several times, she had to hit the brakes of the slick sedan hard when drivers failed to properly approach Savannah's squares.

The minutes marched closer and closer to four and she wasn't in place yet. Summer acknowledged the anticipated spike in anxiety, the increased beat of blood beneath her skin. It had been a while, the physical side effects of engaging in criminal activity rusted yet sharp. But still unnervingly familiar. Maybe she hadn't come as far as she would like to think.

And still no response from Reyes. Initially feeling dismissed, she figured whatever he was caught up with was more important because he would want to know everything that had spiraled out of hand in the last thirty minutes. Considering the man wanted to know every time Jerrod breathed weird—or she repositioned herself while on his couch.

Gratefully, there was a break in the flow of cars, so Summer was able to navigate the remaining distance to the warehouse in Carver Heights with dwindling interference. Adjacent to the railroad area, this slice of town was starkly defined by commercial space and the only residential options were the less than desirable kind. But its lack of appeal mattered little because she had made it here on time.

Waiting for Cameron to emerge was a practice in sheer torture. There had been no further communication from the burner number, nothing from the FBI. She refrained from checking her work email, refused to scroll through a news feed. She forced herself to stay suspended in the moment, ready to act when necessary, unwilling to let any fraction of normalcy leak into this aberration of a situation. She wouldn't constitute her actions as acceptable; they would hold no true tie to her actual life.

Those were the mental affirmations that kept her semi-steady until precisely six and a half minutes after four o'clock when she watched Cameron slide out of a set of metal doors on the left side quadrant of a nondescript building.

He strolled toward her, as if he had all the time in the world, a compact computer bag casually slung over one shoulder. She sincerely doubted it contained what it was intended for. But more importantly, she did *not* want to know what it was being used to cloak.

As images of their final rendezvous came alive, reason battled with reaction, despite all attempts to block out the day she learned her baby was a girl...

Elated, she drove straight home, hoping that though Jerrod provided a valid reason for missing the ultrasound appointment, had decided to leave work early. She hadn't questioned, even though the hurt was a bubbly, messy mass inside her chest. Didn't he want to find out together whether they were going to have a boy or a girl? They'd already picked names, though she secretly wished for a girl. Her perfect little Keira Grace.

The Summer she was then processed his excuse as reasonable though who knew if it had been true, just like everything else she would come to question. She had believed what he wanted her to believe for far too long, a dynamic that would eventually leave her feeling lost and inept and ashamed.

Perhaps if she could have been more honest with herself, she would have persisted with probing deeper because the cracks were already evident, their marriage already crumbling. But she was pregnant—and thrilled to be a mom. Things were only going to get better once the baby came—and she believed he would do the right thing.

But you can't will someone else's potential into practice. You can't cover foundational fissures with pretty wrappings and pink hued bows.

Despite the pain and embarrassment she'd felt from his absence, afterward she returned to their apartment, sonogram photos ready to be shown off, only to be summoned back to EarthScapes.

And she'd gone, dutiful wife, martyr of a sister. Two roles which she had since resoundingly tried to bury. The black and white images of Keira were tucked away for a celebration that would never come, like a permanently suspended dream.

She'd assumed there be time later to rejoice, once the job was done.

After all, Jerrod—and Katelyn—needed her.

Handling the instructions in stride, she maintained the same level head she always did when going on a job, even if internally she was close to bursting with light over her baby girl. Leaving EarthScapes as though nothing had changed, she drove to the site and waited for Cameron.

If it concerned her that they were tangled up in a particularly rough section that skirted city limits, it was only when they were being pursued by the equally rough group of people Jerrod had stupidly chosen to steal from, did that concern explode into terror. She floored that car once Cameron was secured, weaving in and out of side streets, hitting the railroad tracks at a full clip, panicked to end the chase at whatever cost and return everyone home in one piece, despite the blooming pain in her stomach.

And almost everyone was.

All except for the light inside of her soul that became extinguished when, hours later, she had bled out at the hospital, miscarrying her child…

Now, as the same man moved toward her, a false flutter pulsed in her stomach, born of blame, haunted by despair.

"Summer," Cameron greeted her smoothly, shattering the mental images into jagged bits of lethal glass that sliced at her core. "Long time no see."

As though fresh pain wasn't coursing through her, she put the car in reverse and rejoined the flow of commuters pretty damn seamlessly, fighting to stop any grief from leaking out before she released a full breath. "Cameron."

The short reply was not lost on him, but she wasn't interested in pretending to want to make small talk.

"Come on now, it's just like old times."

Seething, she tightened her grip on the wheel, exposing bloodless knuckles. Anger felt warm and welcoming compared to the frigid grasp of memories that demanded to be relived. "It is *not* just like old times, and you sound exactly like him."

"By him, would you be referring to our fearless leader? I thought you two were trying to work something out, hence why you're currently delivering me to the drop spot."

He leaned toward her then, appearing to enjoy watching her stiffen at the increased proximity. "You know, he was bothered about the last time too."

Bothered? Such a pale term by comparison.

"Don't," she flipped up her hand, desperate to end the exchange before it could take root. "Just don't, okay?"

"Okay, okay. Not trying to dredge up the past."

But that's exactly what he was doing, muddying the waters and making the difficult swim to the surface of sanity even more cloudy and disorienting.

It was torturous enough simply seeing Cameron and repeating the act that led to her pregnancy loss, but to hear him put a voice to it, to speak of it so callously and claim Jerrod held anything other than measured indifference—it was too much.

One by one, she released each of those whitened fingers, shifting her grip on the wheel. "You're right, it's in the past. So, leave it alone."

The finality of the statement brought about a stilted silence which lasted until she reached their second destination. This time she didn't even park, merely came to a brief stop only long enough for Cameron to exit. Then, as he was about to shut the door and get scarce, she asked, "What's in the bag?"

It appeared to catch him by surprise as well because he halted for a second before looking back at her with a level of incredulity. "He really didn't tell you?"

Summer gave a slight shake of her head, her cheeks flushing a bit.

"Not my deal then," he said. "But it's interesting, very interesting, I'll give you that."

Before she could ask anymore, he, along with the forsaken bag, disappeared from view. God *damn* it. Fists balled up tight once more before she felt the depletion of energy and her hands slacked against the leather.

Why had she opened her mouth and drawn attention to herself? Why couldn't she have just let the door shut without a word and leave it alone? Knowing the contents of the bag, understanding just how hot the hot goods were, would give her no greater sense of stability. He would tell Jerrod she'd asked, that she hadn't remained objective and dutifully on course. A rogue sheep with no real design on returning to the flock.

With perspective lost and nothing gained, Summer watched Cameron walk away as though he possessed zero cares, arrogance personified, in a world gone mad. Because of her memories, because of everything Cameron had revived, it foolishly took her a few extended minutes to shift the car into drive. It was never wise to linger at a location unless expressly instructed to wait for a designated length of time. But wisdom wasn't exactly the description for today's antics.

But the job was done, and it had, speaking to logistics, been executed without error. Jerrod would see that at least. Only time would show if her actions fostered greater trust and a dynamic that could illuminate on something of value for the FBI's benefit.

As far as Cameron's instigation attempts went…Summer's mental reel hit a hard pause when she heard her phone vibrating inside of the cupholder. Flicking her eyes down to witness the stream of texts scrolling in from Reyes reminded her that the FBI app was still on. How nice that he must have clued in that something was going down, even though it was too late now.

Regardless, she needed to get the hell of out the railroad district and respond to him before anything else happened. But she was already in motion, anonymously rejoining the herd of drivers, leaving the undoubtedly irritating responses unread for the time being.

Her blend into traffic must not have been

anonymous enough because Summer only made it through two intersections before she caught red and blue lights flashing through the rearview mirror.

Her pulse screeched to the wail of the siren.

This could not be happening. Terror tingled, woven with disbelief.

Never, at any point during her marriage to Jerrod and participation in his deals, had she ever encountered police on the job. Despite the fact that her hands had never touched hot goods personally, they were painted just as red as any other member of Jerrod's team. And her luck had just run out.

Adrenaline pumped through her like a drug, tightening her hands against the wheel and setting her heart to race. She slid over to the curb and crept into a parallel spot, the lights flashing behind her in a relentless, intimidating rhythm. It was only now, she realized with horror, that she had no purse, no license, nothing but her phone—there had been little time to think of those pesky things in the middle of her moral crisis outside of Longtime Sun.

Now that oversight became instantly damning.

She cut the engine and waited for several agonizing seconds before the officer finally approached her window. But instead of asking for her license and insurance, his terse command was unexpected. "I need you to keep your hands where I can see them."

Summer slowly blinked. "What? Why?"

How could he have deduced that quickly that she was a member of a sought-after theft ring? Nobody could have ratted her out that fast, yet he was treating her like a viable threat.

"I repeat, keep your hands on the wheel. No

movement!"

She was about to ask another question when he added, "This vehicle has been stolen."

Chapter Ten

Summer hadn't seen Reyes since the morning he had sat in her kitchen and cooked her breakfast, trying to pry personal information out of her. Since he'd left her burning hot enough that, despite the embarrassment and regret, she'd still thought about his mouth long after it had left hers.

So, when he entered the precinct where she currently waited, sending out swirling clouds of temper in his wake, instinct had her recoiling. She straightened her back as he approached, bracing for whatever was about to come.

Noticing her reaction and not caring who watched, he swooped down, pressed his lips to her ear and growled, "Trust me, Ms. Halley, it isn't me you need to be bothered about at the moment."

Just as quickly, he withdrew the same mouth she couldn't stop thinking about, replacing the unquenchable heat with a deflated flood of cool quiet. Striding over to the desk, he scarcely proceeded to flash his badge before being escorted around the corner and out of her sightline. The display seemed quite unnecessary, considering his demeanor screamed authority and few would question the notion that he was in charge.

Summer slumped back down in the chair.

Lack of communication over her fate was excruciating. They'd taken her phone and placed her in a holding cell until Reyes had announced he was on his way. Not in so many words to her, of course, but to some other official in the precinct who understood that his name held weight. Only after she'd been informed of her rescuer's impending arrival had they allowed her to bide there without barriers. His influence had garnered results, good or bad—unlike her efforts.

It was impossible to talk your way out of driving a stolen vehicle no matter how many times you insist you didn't know it was hot.

Any other questions the arresting officer posed swarmed in and out of her mind like bees, their droning stirring up quite the headache. Jerrod's conditioning served her well in the end—Summer succeeded in keeping her mouth shut. But she also needed a miracle, and if salvation came dressed in dark suited authority, so be it.

Their hiatus in the mysterious back room thankfully didn't last long. When Reyes reemerged with the sergeant, Summer was stunned to hear the announcement of her release being made into *his* custody. Not free and clear, only shifting possession to the FBI.

When she shot him a look, wordlessly begging for explanation, he volleyed one right back, making his wishes clear: she needed to keep her mouth shut.

Apparently, that meant all the way out of the station where she was then hustled into an undercover car. Even then, it took him more time to initiate an opening and Summer processed that he was steadying himself before blasting her.

Eventually, "Fucking hell, Ms. Halley!" cleared the way for conversation.

"Hey, I called you as soon as I found the car. *You*

were the one who was impossible to get ahold of. I did my duty."

"Boy, you did. And then some."

When he didn't continue, she countered, "Didn't you read the texts I sent? I told you what was going on. Mostly. That's why you came, is it not?"

He grunted a sound that mimicked agreement.

"Thought so. It's not like you wouldn't have wanted to know. And from the look of it, you're taking me straight home so I can fill you in on all the gruesome details."

Another grunt of approval. When they slowed to a red light, Reyes shifted in the seat. His rigid posture illuminated the seriousness of his mood. "This is not a game, damn it. Now we've let the local PD in on the fact that we've got presence here. Unbelievably, that's not a good thing."

His earlier comments about his father flashed through her mind, causing Summer to shove down some of her hostility. But she hadn't asked to get pulled over. She hadn't coerced Jerrod into roping her into anything. In fact, she felt completely out of control, but that loss didn't necessarily mean Reyes wasn't right. "I do believe you."

Another pointed pause. "There's a statement that must have been quite difficult for you to spit out."

"Precisely, but it's still true."

Then, after a few more awkward moments passed, "What took you so long?"

He sent her a look that was indecipherable, before exhaling and running a hand through his hair. "I was busy petitioning to the team about how useful you could continue to be for us. That meeting was for your benefit,

Ms. Halley. How was I to know Metzinger would up the ante while I was otherwise occupied with defending you?"

"I have yet to see the upside, *Agent Reyes*," she muttered. "Thanks, by the way, for getting me out. And for defending me, as it were."

"No problem, it was necessary."

That comment had her lapsing into a brooding silence that persisted for the remainder of the car ride. She hadn't expected to want to thank him, but the further they got away from the police station, the greater her sense of having dodged a rather lethal bullet. Focusing on that, rather than the novel revelation that he was sticking up for her to what sounded like another viable enemy, still left her with much to dissect.

No phones pinged, no sideways remarks were dropped. Neither she nor Reyes were interested in flinging barbs, which only added to an already disconcerting afternoon. If they weren't bickering, then what would they talk about?

Certainly not the lip lock. With limited success, Summer kept her gaze mostly forward, fixating on what little pleasure she could derive from watching Savannah's historic district whir past.

Once they were back at her place, she took the time she needed to erase the temporary stains of being held custody. At least the physical ones. Inside, Summer tried to push aside the formidable distress over being arrested. Humiliation was an understatement.

She showered, scrubbing herself down with mildly scalding water, then dressed in leggings and an oversized shirt. Hair still damp and face clear of makeup, she reluctantly returned to the living room, figuring private time was pretty much up.

Big and purposefully assuming, Reyes stood in the corner, watching her walk toward him with an intensity far greater than what she'd anticipated. Crossing her arms defensively over her chest, Summer braced herself for the anger she'd witnessed earlier, certain it was ready to reemerge and seek the most likely target—her.

But strangely, he averted his gaze as she got closer, as though he finally realized he was staring. Hard. She mentally willed him to start talking, to put the focus somewhere else, anywhere else.

He took the hint, stiffly gesturing for her to sit with him at the table, even if she wanted more distance. But without an alternative, she sat, watching him out of the corner of her eye. Wrapped up tight, most of his muscles flexed and clenched like he was exercising an amazing amount of self-control just by being beside her. What was harder to determine was whether his tension was born out of disdain...or something else.

Only once they were faced, eye to eye, did he speak again. "I need you to walk me through step by step what happened today. Again, what might seem like a small, insignificant detail, may be crucial. I underestimated this move, should have been ready for him to pull some kind of stunt like this," he added more softly, with a hiss of self-criticism. "But now that he has, it's imperative that we're brought up to speed."

"Okay."

She drew in a breath, began the rundown. "I got to the clinic at my usual time—nine this morning—to set up for longer patient hours since it's Thursday. We were steady, kind of crazy busy actually, but I have Ayana scheduled for the peak check in times before she heads to her night class."

"You brought her on recently?"

"About two months ago. She can only give me part time hours, but it really helps on days like today."

His question temporarily interfered with her train of thought, so when she paused, he motioned for her to continue.

"Anyway, it was Ayana who pointed out that a car had been sitting in one of our spots for a long time without any sign of someone actually getting out or being there for a walk-in appointment. I'm not really one to call for a tow, I'm too busy to worry about that stuff, but we get so little designated parking on the street that it's really irritating when someone misuses it."

She felt his eyes steady on her face and knew he was reading her expressions just as thoroughly as the events themselves. It couldn't matter though, let him watch her. For this part at least, she had nothing to hide. "Once I finished removing the needles from my last two patients, I went out to investigate the vehicle."

"Was anyone still in the clinic by the point or were you by yourself?"

"Ayana was there, finishing some cleaning. The final two appointments left as I was standing outside."

His brows furrowed, unveiling criticism and it raised her hackles. "Listen, I no longer have to run things by someone before I do them. I don't need a keeper."

"I wasn't insinuating—"

"Sure you were and it's irrelevant. I wouldn't have thought to text you before going to look at a car in my own damn parking lot, thank you."

"Maybe not me, but someone. Or at least have Ayana cover you in case there was a problem. Which there was," he murmured.

His concern over her looking at the car by herself seemed misplaced.

"Well, I looked, I drove, I got arrested. Sorry to inconvenience everyone as a result. Believe it or not, I live a relatively quiet life now—or did until quite recently—and don't expect an ambush or something harrowing to accost me at the clinic. Besides, Ayana knows how to lock up and I'll be going back this evening to double check everything anyway," she emphasized, although that felt like stating the obvious. She was never not the last one out the door, even with Ayana knowing the closing process. Control freak, hyper vigilance. They were close cousins of surviving the hustle.

"You should expect the unexpected from now on."

"Understood." It would not be a mistake she cared to relive.

"How did you figure out the stolen car was Metzinger's doing? Or that it was meant for you?"

"Because it was in my parking lot and while I was out there, Jerrod texted with instructions."

"Convenient," he replied. "Mind if I see?"

"Not at all. And by the way—again—I did not know it was stolen until I got pulled over."

She'd been waiting for him to ask to see the texts. There was nothing in the thread that would indicate she had suspected Jerrod of leaving the vehicle sooner in the day. Even before she had set her sights on the stolen sedan, alarm bells had been ringing about possibilities. She just hadn't known the depth of this set up.

Producing her phone, she handed it over, this time turning the tables by studying his face for a reaction. Lips pressed into a tight line, he scrolled through the messages in silence. She knew what made them compress even further before he flicked his gaze back up to her, accentuating those already hardened cheekbones into a deeper scowl. "Why is it, that you felt compelled to let him know of your arrest? So compelled, in fact, to inform him before telling me?"

Suddenly, he was up, pacing the length of her kitchen and stirring up that anger she'd braced for. Summer watched his back, the ripple and rise of strong shoulder blades constricting as the palpable energy struggled to find a release. Whatever tiny hope existed that he wouldn't notice the timetable was obliterated, though hoping for that was like a fool's wish because the man missed nothing. Including that clearly disturbing information that she had notified Jerrod before him.

Whatever obscured reasons for the decision felt sticky and smothering, blanketing the need to be honest with herself. As calmly as she could, she pretended to study her nonexistent manicure. "Did you expect me not to tell him? Don't you think that would have looked suspicious to keep my mouth shut?"

When he didn't immediately respond, she figured he must agree on some level. But the prowling continued, the shifting temper still flowed. "Trust me, it would have looked way worse if I had kept it to myself. Even if I had been charged, had the car seized and attempted to deal with the entire mess on my own, Jerrod still would have found out anyway. Somehow, he always knows. And." She got to her last point by raising her voice, "You *should* have known what was going on first. I texted you before I even got in the car."

His body went still as though her statement was an accusation. "That you did," he acknowledged with a deceptive amount of calm. "But I'm talking about when the authorities got involved. That news was shared with me long after you updated Metzinger."

"All I did was send him the code word for trouble, I didn't tell him anything specific—"

"I know what a code word means, Ms. Halley."

With that, he approached the table again before pivoting away as though he thought better of it. Turning to give her his back, his arms folded, presumably checking his phone or attending to some other official business. Either way, she was effectively dismissed.

"I bet you do," she spoke lowly, sifting through the uncomfortable sensation that she had somehow let Reyes down. Was he back to questioning her motives again? Weighing out how clear her conscious was? Probably still debating about how dirty her hands were even after defending her. Even after what happened between them…

Guilt spread like black tar, coating her chest and reminding her of everything she'd worked so hard to undo. The sensation wasn't new, but she couldn't help feeling perplexed over the unclear reason she'd chosen to tell Jerrod first. Had purposefully done so. Perhaps there was something intrinsically twisted about her, knowing that she would align with a known enemy instead of a hesitant ally.

In defense against Reyes' uncanny ability to read her face, Summer averted her eyes once he rejoined her at the table. For a split second in her periphery, she processed his eyes snagging on her mouth, dropping lower, before shuttering down to seal away any emotion.

When she finally looked into that impenetrable expression of stone, it served as a glaring reminder that she should not consider him an ally. They were not on the same side. Venturing with caution, she asked, "Did the cops trace the car?"

"Don't worry about your ex, he's got himself well shielded. Last I heard, while the vehicle was being impounded, the owner claimed that he forgot he'd lent the car to a friend, then accidentally reported it stolen. Went on record with such lies. He's coming to collect it, no harm no foul, after the red tape clears. Once again, Metzinger was able to slide out of it."

"Well then, it sounds like the whole thing got wrapped up nicely for everyone."

"You can save the sarcasm, we're not done yet. There's still some unaccounted time to go over. I'd like your version before things are…speculated over by the bureau."

"The time when I was driving?"

"Drive time there, to the drop site and then up until you got pulled over," he confirmed.

Summer gave the rundown as systematically as possible, omitting her spiking nerves and the way Cameron had tried—and succeeded—to provoke her.

Reyes interjected now and again, asking her to clarify or expand. When she got to Cameron's entrance on the scene, his demeanor sharpened. "When you say it was a computer bag, what kind? Shoulder strap, backpack?"

"Shoulder strap, relatively on the small side. Compact enough that I can't figure out what they were after or even get a solid impression of size or shape. But I know he got it—Cameron, I mean."

"He told you that? Confirmed it?"

"I know him…well enough to know when he's

executed the job. I know he got it because he was acting arrogant."

Reyes appeared to ponder that insight for a moment before asking, "Why do you hate him so much?"

Paling, her eyes darted across his face then away. "You must know by now how I feel about arrogant men," she quipped but the attempt to sound brazen and unaffected failed. Reyes merely waited, arms crossed, for her to ditch the attitude and continue.

Slowly Summer unclenched fists she hadn't known she'd been gripping. Doing a swift, internal scan, she loosened muscles where she could, willing herself to be steady before asking, "What makes you think I hate him?"

"Everything about the way you say his name, the way you speak about whatever history you two have shared."

"History. I guess that's one way to put it. It's certainly in the past and is in no way relevant to right now so why does it matter?"

"I'm trying to understand you more," he said quietly after a moment.

"Oh."

It was tough to stay neutral when he talked to her like that. Instincts had her pushing back while her head toyed with the idea that it could be okay to hedge the truth and still give a little. "He witnessed something very personal that happened on a job one time."

"Very personal? With you?"

"Yes."

He was watching her in a nearly identical way to when he had stood beside her desk at the clinic, perceiving the anguish, yet unaware of its source. The shifting that occurred inside the cold place in her chest did not move comfortably. Summer brushed the tips of her fingers across her sternum, willing the pressure to settle the broken bones comprising her heart.

She didn't anticipate when he moved closer, only registered that he was beside her seconds before his hand raised. Raw awareness blistered the air but despite the tension, he withheld actual contact as his hand curved in a phantom caress near her jaw line. Breath suspended, the hand at her chest flexed from wanting to seek his out, to soak in his warmth. For that alone, she told herself she would remain stubbornly still.

"It's okay, Summer. You don't have to tell me."

And suddenly she was no longer Ms. Halley but an actual person. It worked, wearing down those walls of self-preservation. "Thank you," she whispered, feeling herself give in a little. Too much. Not enough.

Releasing a bit of the control she kept, she brought her fingertips up to graze across his knuckles, returning his almost touch with a featherlight stroke across smooth, warm skin. Relishing the impact, the implied act of comfort, even as it began to morph into something more. A resonating pulse began to throb, seeking, building, and when she would have sought more, he sharply withdrew his hand as if her touch had seared him.

The warmth she'd captured vanished and along with it, her resolve. Tears threatened to spill as Summer refused to look at him, hating herself for the split second where she'd forgotten that he would hurt her. That he had the capacity to bruise the things inside that were already long broken.

All these games and all this deceit would be her undoing if she let them. So weary of all the manipulation, she recognized a kind of deep, exhausted sorrow sinking down into her bones.

In the effort it took to avoid his scrutiny—if he even cared to look back—she was slow to notice when he slipped away without saying anything else.

By the time she acknowledged his departure, she also registered the click of the front door closing. Locking. Shutting her eyes, she worked to accept that she was once again alone.

Told herself it was absolutely for the best.

Chapter Eleven

Jerrod waited a solid twenty-four hours before responding to her emergency code word. And even then, the cryptic text—sent from yet another burner number—sounded like his only worry was covering tracks with the stolen vehicle stunt, not about her brush with the law. From what Reyes disclosed, she knew Jerrod's damage control was laced in shit. He'd already intercepted the vehicle owner, bought off whomever necessary to prevent exposure. Probably before she had even touched the steering wheel.

By that time, Reyes and the team had put in extensive hours retracing the path she'd relayed, only to report what was already suspected: Not a hair out of place, not one scrap of useful evidence to be found and linked to her ex-husband.

Their preoccupation with recreating the getaway instructions meant Reyes would leave her alone for the time being, for which she was thoroughly grateful. But it was becoming increasingly difficult to dodge his questions. By combining an element of compassion with ruthless tenacity, even agreeing to leave certain subjects alone for the interim, he was much closer to gaining ground with her than was wise or comfortable. Whether it had anything to do with the mutual heat she'd captured only slivers of, she didn't want to consider.

Somehow, she would figure out a way to do what everyone needed her to do while preserving the delicate layers of deception that still veiled all sides. But talking about Keira...explaining what happened? Finding transparency with her own family had been nearly impossible. Reyes was a different matter entirely.

After she miscarried Keira, her mom and sister formed a sort of silent ring of support, making it known that they were there and not expecting Summer to talk until she was ready—but she never was.

Their quiet level of love got her through the first parts, the darkest parts, especially in the face of Jerrod's indifference. But after all the ashes eventually blew away, after no one wanted to bring it up anymore, the unrelenting pain continued to spread. Without release, her suffering remained constant, weaving into an integral part of who she now was.

Ultimately, Summer didn't feel worthy of their sympathy. She didn't deserve to be understood, to be comforted. Eventually, enough time passed so that they didn't watch her so intently, and it became easier to assume she had moved beyond her grief.

Which made her momentary consideration to confide in Reyes all the more shocking.

He must be exceptionally good at his job, she reprimanded herself as she powered through the after-hours paperwork that evening.

Right now, he and the team were out trying to nail Jerrod—and to a lesser extent, her—to whatever item, or items, Cameron had stolen. They would fail, which is why they had been desperate enough to enlist her help in the first place. But if the FBI could tighten their grasp around Jerrod, find a way to shine accusation in her direction as well, Summer had no doubt they would use whatever was at their disposal. Reyes defending her usefulness didn't make her any less targeted.

Objectively, she could admire Jerrod's attention to detail, the meticulous approach he took to keep his hidden endeavors thriving. But she wasn't feeling very objective at the moment. Knowing he had his bases covered, he'd left her hanging out there for the police. Even if she had given him up, it would come down to her word against his, leaving her the loser in that equation.

She really, *really* hoped they found something at the scene so she could be put out of her misery, but as the hours went by, hopes of success shrank.

But it was equally hard to view Jerrod as consistently untouchable. He was neither omnipotent nor without weakness. Here she had assumed he was testing her loyalty, all while withholding his own. Yet, he was no more loyal to her than to anyone else on his payroll. The only loyalty that existed was to himself—which she knew, which she'd come to terms with—but had apparently needed this reminder. And that's where the FBI was getting it wrong. She truly held no sway with him. But maybe that was where his weakness still lay, in his blindness to anything that wasn't self-serving. Any narcissist's downfall could be rooted in their vast selfishness.

These were the insightful pieces to the puzzle she should be sharing with the authorities who assumed her unique level of intimacy with Jerrod could elicit more than an outsider working their way in, trying to ferret out weak spots.

Her phone vibrated, jarring her out of her thoughts. Jerrod's regular number scrolled across the screen and sent nausea roiling through her stomach. It took an extraordinary amount of self-discipline to make her swipe it open. Immediately she saw she'd been on target about his attempt to placate with an apology delivered in the singular way he understood. Food, wine and the pleasure of his company.

After agreeing to the proposal—because there was no other choice—Summer set her phone back down and stared into the silence surrounding her.

There was no way. No way out of it all but she would not succumb to where her mind wanted to drag her down and keep her. She was so tired of having everyone else pulling the strings, everyone else—including her own emotions, her own memories—having control.

The quiet was suffocating. To reject feeling so hopeless, , she picked up her phone and clicked on something she hadn't bothered with in months. Online dating was a minefield, one for which she was poorly trained. Likes, swipes, and acronyms she had no desire to decipher. But when she became single, Katelyn created her profile and insisted on showing her how to use the app. She dug into the queue with minimal enthusiasm, tapping matches at random. After a few minutes of scrolling and swiping, a message appeared.

That was faster and easier than she'd thought.

The exchanges she made with an available match were breezy and harmless, with the added bonus of instant distraction. Here was an opportunity to connect with someone outside of everything, the appeal of pretending to be someone else for a little while enticing. Satisfaction was short-lived, however. When maintaining the dialogue grew tedious and reality inevitably bled back into the present, Summer closed out the conversation and breathed. Focusing on drawing one breath in at a time, slow and steady. She focused on the way the oxygen entered her nostrils and the full feeling as it lingered in her lungs.

With less conviction, she placed the call to Reyes before she changed her mind.

"Reyes," he answered gruffly after the first ring, his voice triggering an unexpected spike of exhilaration in her blood, helping to dissolve the steel webs of depression.

"It's me."

"Ms. Halley," he acknowledged in a brisque tone that indicated she was interrupting something.

"Jerrod just reached out."

After she let a few moments of silence stretch, knowing it would irritate him, on cue, he let loose a growly, "And?"

"And he wants to make amends for the unfortunate stolen car incident. I'm going to his place tonight."

His voice elevated, losing its annoyed quality, and he zeroed all of his energy on her. "And how exactly is Metzinger going to make this up to you? Summoning you to participate in another theft?"

"No," she answered succinctly. "This would be his usual method. Wine, good food. Gracing me with his presence."

The following silence over the line was deafening. Finally, a flinty, "I see" punctured the tension.

"Figured you wanted me to keep you informed even though I'm sure nothing about the last job will be discussed because he'll want me to get over it and move on. Hashing it out wouldn't help."

"Most likely not." Reyes' tone was now bordering on abrasive, evoking a matched irritation in response.

"What exactly is your problem? Was this too

mundane to bother you with?"

"Quite the opposite, Ms. Halley."

So, she was back to Ms. Halley. And he was back to being purposefully cryptic. "Okay, better idea. Ignore Jerrod completely and take my match up on his offer of a date."

The static on the line had her checking to see that the call hadn't been dropped. "Dating is not on the agenda," he ground out, confirming his presence and the fact she'd hit a mark.

"Why not?"

"You know perfectly well why not. I don't have time to break it down for you."

She pretended to ponder his nonanswer. "Is it because you're jealous?"

A return to silence, then a snarled, "Your interest should be solely on Jerrod. He's who you need to be flirting with, not some online jackass looking for a quick hookup."

She grinned, wishing they were face to face to see how he worked his way out of this one. "Okay," she replied sweetly. "I'll keep the app running the whole time I'm at *Jerrod's*. Can I expect to see you before I leave?"

He grunted some sort of non-committal response before the line went dead.

Smiling, she rose to finish up the last closing tasks for the clinic with steps that were lighter and a head that was clearer. Needling her resident agent had significantly lifted her mood. Harnessing the power of purpose once she was back home, Summer took an extended amount of time straightening her hair, applying make-up and carefully selecting something that showed off her body. She wasn't being overt, merely strategic. Then, relatively satisfied with the results of her efforts, she locked the door behind her, signaling to Reyes that he was *not* welcome. She could chase her own demons.

****

Two bottles of champagne nestled on ice beside the mimicked fire licking up the inside of the electric insert flanked by stacked stone.

Upon her arrival, Jerrod greeted her at the foyer almost instantly, reaching out to remove her coat, then ushering her over to the cozy, little living room set up he had obviously spent time orchestrating. "Summer," he brushed a kiss against her temple, counteracting the heat that had begun to warm her skin with flurries of repulsion that scurried like ants. "So glad you could make it."

He said this as if the summons and subsequent method of apology appeared voluntary. She knew better. Smiling tightly, she merely lifted her flute to her lips, taking her time to school her face, pretending it wasn't a wasted effort. "Me too. I could use some wine, some company."

It wasn't a lie—she *could* use those things, just in a different location with a different host. Involuntarily thinking of Reyes, wondering where he was and if he was on the receiving end of the listening device, avidly awaiting some vital intel, Summer kicked up the flirt in her tone. "Tell me, did I do everything you needed from me the other day?"

A brief flicker that could have been interpreted as being caught off guard, Jerrod drank deeply before offering her an incline of his chin meant to signify agreement. But she knew him better than most, needed to remember that few would have picked up on the minute flicker of surprise. He assumed she wouldn't be the first to bring up the incident.

Play up his brilliance, show hesitance for her own competence. She could do this. "Sorry, I just haven't been on a job in a while and felt…out of practice."

Any fleeting surprise was quickly replaced with a familiar, arrogant smirk. "Like I said, just like old times. You did everything I needed, like you used to. I knew you would."

Something inside snapped shut while simultaneously a vault of anger was pried open. Fury that couldn't be contained. Summer felt her lips peel back, processed the growl that escaped her throat as though it were happening to somebody else. "If I did everything you needed, then where's my cut?"

Glittering fury answered her own and contorted his face before he replied, smooth as silk, "Darling, I'm not sure you could handle a cut of this."

In the next instant, he was on her, dragging rough hands up her thighs and hips before securing them tight behind her neck. In a move of clear intent and ownership, Jerrod's boldness, executed in a finger snap, galvanized her.

Rendered frozen for several agonizing seconds before some other section of her brain kicked into gear, she scrambled to get into action. To survive.

Returning his embrace was one of the hardest things she had done, but she did it, out of sheer immediacy.

Jerrod's mouth held an achingly familiar taste, one that evoked a myriad of tainted memories. They flooded through her, taking her down in their intensity and when she gasped against his lips, a moan he predictably took as sexual, the raw honesty of it shocked her. It unearthed waves of buried sadness, coupled with that fury, bringing about a renewed revelation of how lasting the impact of their relationship had been.

Her sounds of regret increased the pace of Jerrod's advance, elevating his breathing and drawing Summer back to the present and out of her internal drowning.

Suddenly her dress was shoved aside, her legs nudged open.

Through the blanket of emotions, the continuous ringing of her phone registered that someone was insistent in their effort to reach her.

Pushing a hand against his chest did no good. Jerrod had no intention of stopping.

Shoving harder against that solid expanse of muscle, Summer fought her way into a better sitting position.

"What the fuck, Summer?"

"Sorry…it's just, my phone. I-I need to answer. It could be Katelyn."

His look of disdain revealed the ugliness disguised beneath a surface of charisma. One hand reached out, aggressively cupped the front of her panties before he forcefully pulled the fabric aside, exposing her flesh, violating her with a stare that took what he wanted, watched what he sought. She squeezed her eyes shut against the visual assault.

Then the veneer slid back into place, and he carefully settled the silk back over her flesh and pulled her dress back down as though the intimacy was perfectly normal, mutual and welcomed.

Blood roared in her head as Summer scrambled off the couch and snatched the phone out of her wristlet only to be met with numerous texts and missed calls from the same name, all sent in a very specific time frame.

Desperate breath needed to escape but she squeezed her eyes and lips shut while keeping her back turned. Then she tossed back the rest of the champagne and set the glass down with a quick rap. "I'm so sorry, Jerrod. I've got to go. It's my sister, she needs me."

He watched her with dark, stalking eyes, unfathomably shaded against their usual pale shade. Did he sense her deception? Desperation? Need?

She feared he wouldn't let her go.

With purpose, he closed the space between them and gave her ass a hard, bruising squeeze. "To be continued."

Her breath finally betrayed her, exhaling with relief just as he released his grip. But it was the true threat that followed her home.

Chapter Twelve

Summer found her front door unlocked. *How obliging of him.*

She stomped to the teak entry bench, deposited her keys and turned to find the living room empty, adding fuel to an already simmering fire which she'd gladly stoked during her journey back home.

All for being summoned. Again. He'd blown up her phone, all but called an emergency to get her back here and then…nothing. He's just like Jerrod, her head screamed, herding her like cattle whenever he wished, bidding her to do whatever he deemed was more important at the moment he felt it needed doing.

Furious, relieved and undeniably curious, Summer checked both bedrooms before hurrying through the kitchen galley to the back laundry nook.

No Reyes.

She stood, absorbing the fact he wasn't there waiting for her. Which was a struggle because her head was swimming with champagne and disgust over what Jerrod had done. Would have done if not for the phone calls…

Combined now with her whirling emotions over Reyes, an added level of apprehension emerged the longer she swayed in the silence.

What if something bad was happening? In their short association, Summer had come to doubt Liam Reyes would act frivolously—or on sheer impulse—and certainly not if it involved official FBI business.

Yet, he had just called her out of Jerrod's territory, demanded she immediately return home under the pretense of Katelyn's name and now appeared to be ghosting her.

Anger bubbled up once more, along with a comforting relief that surged to the surface. Summer grabbed her phone, feeding off the negative energy as it worked to keep other unnamed feelings at bay. Blasting out the back door, thumb poised to hit the call button, she pulled up so fast, she nearly lost her footing and stumbled over the cobblestones.

Reyes stood at the far edge of the courtyard, facing away from her. The only movement seen was the rapid rise and fall of his breathing, indicating a significant lack of restraint.

Good. She'd been operating without hers since she left Jerrod's.

Launching toward him, he whipped around before she made contact—exactly what she'd intended if she was able to get her hands on him, Summer wasn't sure. Only that she craved a tangible outlet to her feelings, no matter how unwise.

"Better think again, Ms. Halley."

She let loose a frustrated breath that mimicked a howl and a growl. Yanking her hands down, she clenched them together tightly as she tried to stifle the urge to strike something.

"You can save the Ms. Halley shit," she seethed. "What the hell is going on? You made me think something major was going down, but then you're just out here, doing what? Brooding? *Did* something happen or not?"

"I do not brood. Ms. Halley."

The purposeful use of the formality incited the intended reaction. But even with the obvious provocation, her words stumbled upon seeing his rising level of swirling turbulence. "I-I was working, doing what you wanted me to. Doing what everyone wants me to do—"

She processed that he was crowding her, maneuvering her backward, winding them both deeper into darkness when her hands inadvertently brushed up against the exterior wall of the building. Something was definitely wrong here.

Shrouded in the shadows of the eaves, he imposed his body toward hers, proving once more he could do whatever he wanted, whenever he wanted.

Just like her ex.

"Working. Interesting word choice."

She stood firm. "I was *busy* trying to do the right thing, so if you called me back here to berate me, after telling me to use Katelyn as an out…"

"I heard you," he hissed in a whisper. "On the app."

Of course he'd heard her on the app, wasn't that the point of turning it on?

Dumbfounded, Summer stared into his face a few, ruthless inches from hers. He placed his hands on the wall, bracketing her head, infiltrating her senses.

Her confusion must have been clear because he gave a slight, derisive snort. "Yes, I know; you did what you were supposed to do. You were *working* and then some. It's me who didn't do what was necessary. I'm the one who didn't do what was right."

Slowly, slowly, realization dawned as Summer watched his expressions leak through the anger. He'd *heard* her. As in he'd heard her groans, the same ones Jerrod had mistaken for desire. The ones that exposed her buried suffering while at the same time being torn apart by a kiss that should never have happened.

The ones he had possibly mistaken for desire too...

"You don't understand," she started quickly before hesitating, trying to figure out a way to explain that her vocalizations had been ones of torment, not pleasure.

At her fractured protest, he hastily removed his hands and straightened so sharply, it was as though she'd struck him. With the regained distance, air flowed back into her lungs. The problem was, it felt cold as ice, just as harsh and unrelenting.

"I simply thought to save you from doing something I know you would regret after," he offered in a voice gone frosty. Whatever hot emotions that flowed through him moments ago now appeared doused with frigid indifference.

"You were trying to save me from my ex-husband?" she asked incredulously, trying to keep up with his whiplash reactions. "That doesn't make much sense considering that's the whole point of this assignment, isn't it?"

"I figured you'd be more likely to cooperate in the future if you didn't feel like you were being pimped out to Metzinger."

He was retreating, withdrawing in more ways than just space.

"Reyes, I—"

"Sorry to cut your romantic evening short and make you rush back over here." His voice dripped with impenetrable ice. "I'm sure there will be another time to, ah, follow through with whatever had gotten started. Bad judgement call, all in all. I apologize. You should get some sleep."

Turning on his heel, he crossed the yard in swift strides and Summer yelped, "Wait! Reyes!"

But he gave no heed to her calls, would not even spare a glance back when he disappeared into the house. From the courtyard she heard the slam of the front door. She imagined he'd flipped the lock for good measure, attempting to close her in. Or close her out from the splinter of vulnerability he'd just showed.

What had she done? What had he?

Hugging her arms across her chest, she leaned against the house in nearly the exact same spot where he had just ignited a fire inside her. A fire now diminished to throbbing, unanswered embers.

She could wallow in it; she could yield to his rejection. Or, she decided, she could get some fucking answers.

****

Movement didn't come easily at first, but then she was racing out the side gate, cutting the distance to the street. Summer managed to catch a glimpse of him as he reached the crosswalk at the end of the street before disappearing between a row of city trees thriving amid sections of cracked concrete. She considered how she never actually knew how he traveled to and from her house, never having seen him park a vehicle out front. It appeared that wherever his ride was kept, it was far enough away to have bought her some time.

"Reyes!" Her voice boomed out on the street side where, for a weekday night, things were eerily hushed. She tried to ignore the cringe worthy quality of the noise she made and shouted again.

This time, her piercing call suspended his progress long enough for her to catch up before he had the chance to turn the corner. His gaze sliced through her. Eyes like amber orbs glared hot but she didn't let that slow her down. "Reyes."

By this time, she was relatively steady—then it all exploded. "I thought this is what you all wanted. What you demanded of me. You put me up to this whole thing, even suggested using my assets, we'll call them, to my advantage. But then you pulled me out? Pulled me back without a reason? Tell me why!"

"To save your ass."

She snorted. "Yeah, I'm sure it was my ass you were thinking of when you approached me. I'm sure it's my ass you're thinking of now. Don't delude yourself into thinking—"

"God damn it, Summer, it's always your ass that I'm thinking about. To a point where I can't think straight!"

The statement landed like a bomb, silencing both sides of the yelling match.

She couldn't help the reaction, because for some sadistic reason, it felt like a victory. He finally, *finally* admitted he found her attractive. A triumphant smile tugged at her lips which only incited another snarl. "This changes nothing. You get that? I've got a job to do. So do you."

"Yes, as you have reminded me. Repeatedly. I get it. *Reyes.*"

"If you get it like you claim, then you should also get why I have to go. You're wasting your time now."

"Am I? Is that your excuse for what's happening between you and me? A waste of time?"

"Yes. It's late, you're back, and there's no point in

my being here now."

"Then why are you?"

For a heightened moment, she thought he looked like he was about to change his mind and say something else but instead, he ended up striding away, leaving her standing at the corner like he apparently intended to from the beginning. This time she let him go. It was embarrassing enough to have chased him down once, she certainly wouldn't do it again.

Regardless, it took some time before she made her way back inside. The decline in their mutually generated friction left her hollow and exhausted. The whole evening left her hollow and exhausted, though it seemed ages since Jerrod nearly assaulted her on his couch.

Once settled in bed, cocooned in absolute darkness, she deliberately left no room for contemplation. Jerrod had been right about one thing—she hated sleeping alone, in an empty house, without comfort. It was something she hadn't realized affected her so significantly until she no longer had a person to sleep beside.

Willing her eyes to close, Summer forced her brain to empty. She would sleep and recharge and be ready to conquer whatever got thrown at her tomorrow. The proof lay in the choices she'd made and would continue making since she had taken back control of her life.

Summer did not need anybody but herself.

****

—*You won't get away with it*—

The anonymous text greeted her upon waking, chilling the spirit she'd attempted to recharge after the catastrophic night with Jerrod, then Reyes.

Rereading it, scrutinizing it, was pointless. Only

that, less and less, did she believe Jerrod was behind the menacing messages. She was also starting to think she should tell Reyes, except, no way after what had gone down last night.

So, instead, the message remained unanswered within the growing collection of mystery numbers.

Chapter Thirteen

When a knock unexpectedly sounded shortly after she arrived home from Longtime Sun the following afternoon, Summer instantly braced herself for whatever conflict was about to erupt.

Shock was an understatement when she opened the door and found, instead of combat, two of her favorite people. "Surprise!"

Admittedly taken aback, it took her several beats to process that the swelling happiness was also riddled with disappointment.

"See, Mom?" Katelyn interjected. "We should've texted first."

"And ruin a perfectly good ambush? No way."

"Excuse me," Summer chimed in, "want to let me in on what you're ambushing me for? And by the way, when did you get in, Mom?"

"Girl's night," they replied in unison.

"I got in late last night after Katelyn's coaxing," her mother said, one hand raised to halt any protest. "Before you can reason with us as to why that's not a good idea, your sister is feeling good this week—which is reason enough to celebrate. And you have been working so hard at the clinic—another valid reason to celebrate. So," she finished proudly. "Girls' night."

With a genuine smile blooming on her face, and trying to embrace the positive vibes, Summer stepped aside to let her family in. "Okay. Give me a few minutes and then girls' night is on."

Rooftop lounges were yet one more reason she loved Savannah.

Someone could take in a greater expansive view afforded from the higher elevation. The tops of buildings, each with their own distinctive shape, were determined by the vastly varying architecture prevalent throughout the city. The scope of history was highlighted by trails of differing illumination, their unique glows increasing with the falling dusk.

Gravitating toward a tower heater, the round table they gathered at was one of many situated on the faux turf accentuating the top deck of the bar.

The three women took little time perusing the menu, a unanimous decision made to go with bubbles. It was refreshing to be on the same page as those in her company, given the last disastrous episode with Katelyn.

Accepting that her sister did appear to be feeling better and was acting uncharacteristically accommodating, went a long way to setting her mood back on solid ground. And seeing her mom, looking so damn pleased with herself for pulling off the surprise visit.

For all those reasons and more, it was beyond ridiculous to feel disappointment over it not being Reyes at her door. They owed each other nothing. It was imperative that she keep that logic in place and squarely in the forefront of her mind. Right now the only thing she intended to focus on was thoroughly enjoying the evening ahead.

Once the champagne was chilling and the appetizers had been ordered, the conversation revived itself. "I still can't believe you came up here, Mom. Last time we talked, you were floating on a board in the Atlantic Ocean."

Emily smiled. "I do love my new class. We meet every Sunday."

"That's so great, and…brave. How hard is it to stand up?"

"Easier to stand, but harder to stay there. Plus, I've got a great teacher and sometimes we grab lunch after class at this little oceanside café."

There it was, an inkling about the source of her mother's modesty. Whoever was instructing the class was quite possibly causing her mother to blush.

Then the silliness cleared, abruptly dampened by some unknown cloud and both her mom and sister sat up a little straighter, a tactic that occurred in unison. "There is something Katelyn and I would like to express our concern about, Summer."

Resentful that the cloud of concern could darken their enjoyment, eyes narrowed she asked, "What is this, like an intervention?"

"I told you, I was going to respect your privacy for only so long before demanding answers about that…man. Time's up, buttercup," Katelyn said. "Why Jerrod? Why do this to yourself all over again?"

Swallowing hard at her sister's directness, Summer shifted her eyes back over to Emily, only to register the same persistence clear in blue eyes nearly the exact shade as her own. Blaming others wouldn't do. This was turbulence of her own making. Mentally scrambling to come up with something tangible enough to satisfy, Summer popped in a toast point then wet her throat with champagne to buy time.

"It's like I told you," she offered weakly. "We missed each other and are trying things out again, seeing where it goes. On different terms, I guess, but still. Just a trial…"

That answer was met with justified skepticism, an eye roll from Katelyn and a measured look of disapproval from Emily.

It was her mother who spoke next, in a quietly resolute tone. "Summer, it's natural to feel lonely after a divorce and certainly after everything you went through. Needing someone is very normal and you have a lot to offer somebody. We're just concerned. There were many valid reasons why you made the decision you did. A decision that you knew was the right one then. Is it the right one now?"

If only they knew the depth of it—and the truth of it. Shame burned bitterly in her chest. "I know it was right for me then, but this is now and maybe…I was wrong." The words were so abhorrent, she wanted to choke on the revolting lies. But if she indeed wanted to do better, there was no choice but to stick with the ruse.

"And I don't *need* someone," Summer added pointedly, desperate not to sound like she lacked a spine. "I have my own business, I run my own life."

"You do," her mom agreed. "You've poured your heart and soul into your clinic, but that doesn't mean that's all there can be for you. It doesn't mean you have to settle on what's comfortable or familiar."

"I take it you two have discussed the matter at length and both agree I'm doing the wrong thing with my current choice of companionship?" Her voice sounded colder now, icier, but it was preferable to the shameful heat that clogged her throat.

In a slice of a second, Katelyn's face cracked, exposing something akin to remorse. Her sister didn't need to feel guilty over her concern. If the roles were reversed, Summer would do the same. In her mind, it wasn't betraying sibling loyalty by confiding in their mother. Emily was their Switzerland. Their probing drove her to refill her glass at a steady pace, earning a few additional sideways looks from both Emily and Katelyn.

But eventually the need for defense eased as the topic turned away from her ex-husband catastrophe and found its way toward Katelyn's latest radiation round and Emily's new Pilates class.

Through a fuzzy, comforting champagne haze, Summer leaned back and became enthralled with people watching. The variety of patrons ebbed and flowed between the heaters and couches, forming pods of social groups or intimate pairings of two. It was distracting in a safe way, putting attention toward strangers she would likely never see again and didn't expect anything from her. After a while, someone's shape outlined near the bar captured her focus. Someone whose face was shadowed beneath the awning yet moved with an unnerving familiarity that sent tingles rushing down her arms. Involuntarily shivering, Summer sucked breath in through her teeth, unable to look away.

Apparently having kept a watchful eye on her, Katelyn instantly homed in on the audible inhale before turning around to follow Summer's sightlines over to the bar. "Summer. Damn, do you know him?"

Did she fricking know him?

In the instant their eye contact collided, the mutual acknowledgement of each other's presence amplified the invisible threads of electricity streaking through the air. He immediately rose, abandoning the coveted stool that was swiftly claimed upon vacancy, and began weaving through the crowd, making his destination clear. He was coming right for them. For her.

Once the distance was closed, and Reyes stood before their table, served up like on a fucking platter, all three females addressed him with riveted attention. "Summer, so good to see you. And ladies," he commented smoothly before depositing himself into the fourth chair. "I hope I'm not interrupting…"

The deliberate pause gave leeway to her family to ruin any chances of her getting out of this one. Not that she had devised an escape route with the wine and sexual tension swirling madly in her head. And from the covert grins and unabashed admiration, Summer deduced she wasn't the only one reeling from the tall, alluring package that had just been dropped into the mix.

"Not at all," Katelyn declared, a little too enthusiastically. "So, you, uh, you know my sister?"

"I do, yeah. I'm a client of Summer's, a fairly new one, in fact. Nice to see a familiar face." He offered up a brilliant smile and a hand to Emily. "Liam."

He lied so fluently, with such practiced precision, Summer felt a flush of nausea roll through her fog of disbelief. To keep everything where it was supposed to be, she polished off the remaining champagne then gulped some water while he enraptured her mom and sister with conversation.

If anyone was picking up on the fact that she did not want *Liam* at the table—or noticed that she had not spoken a single word since he sat down and wrecked her peace, no one commented. Meanwhile, he was busy painting some fallacy of a picture about having recently moved to Georgia and stumbling upon Longtime Sun as some sort of saving grace to his relocation stress.

It sounded laughably on point, like the entire situation could have been perfectly plausible. And all the while, her mother and sister showered him with positive questions, literally eating him up.

"I need the bathroom," she announced ungraciously, suddenly unable to not get up and move away from the situation. While the initial nausea had subsided, her overall mood had rapidly deteriorated. It seemed prudent to remove herself before she could no longer control her tongue.

With as much dignity as she could muster, Summer beelined it to the far side of the bar, hoping the shadows would serve to hide her while she fought for slices of collectedness.

But Reyes didn't take the hint.

He appeared beside her what felt like only moments later, running a hand along her arm. "Are you feeling sick?" he murmured.

"Am I feeling sick?" she parroted, fighting the sway toward his touch, like some sort of self-destructive gravitational pull. "You're crashing my girls' night, flirting with my family and flat out lying about our association. I guess *sick* is one way to describe how I feel."

"Would you rather I tell them the real reason of our acquaintance?"

"I would rather you not be here at all!"

His face was distorted by the minimal lighting, but she could have sworn he flashed a shit eating grin. "Is that right? You would rather I not be here at all?"

"Yes!"

"See, I don't believe that for a second. And since your lovely mother and sister think I'm charming, I know they won't mind me sticking around."

She wanted to maul him, take him down and claw his eyes out. She was then struck with an uncontrollable urge to laugh. This latest version of Liam Reyes didn't hit true with the man on the street the other night. The one whose rejection was swift and calculating, who chose when she was Summer or Ms. Halley to him, depending on the mood.

Succumbing to a fit of hysteria—the alternative was to cry, she released a sequence of stress-relieving laughs. "Of course they think you're charming," she managed when the spasms subsided. "You could make a corpse work up a visceral response if that was your goal."

His grin widened. "That's the spirit. Now, try to remember how captivating I am when we walk back over together. Not corpse like, but as if we're newly, but mutually friendly. You know, as though you don't despise me and I'm a valued client grateful to be in your thoughtful care. I'm saving you here. Again."

The words, just as they had the other night, dug in hard. Resigned, Summer gave a semi-convincing nod of consent and allowed her self-appointed savior to lead the way back to the table. Stumbling slightly once they came into view, Liam made a bit of a show out of helping steady her gait.

Balking at the unnecessary assistance—she was only moderately tipsy, not falling down drunk—a swift but unmistakable look of warning flashed in his eyes, urging her not to disagree with the gesture of gallantry.

The warning stayed with her while Katelyn's eyes

tracked her movements back into the chair, then slid over to Reyes and back again. Distinct humor lit her eyes. In a mock whisper, she leaned toward Summer, "If I didn't know better, I'd say you're setting up for some deliciously well-deserved revenge."

Mortified, Summer stared at her sister. She was no cheater, no matter how much she might despise Jerrod. "I, uh, no….it's not like that, um." This time it was her words that stumbled and of their own accord, her eyes locked with Reyes' again, seeking assistance.

Picking up on her silent cue, he seamlessly explained, "She's had a bit too much to drink. I can make sure she gets back home safely—if she'd like."

"Yeah…" she agreed slowly, digesting the reality of how asking him for help might end up. "I should probably call it a night."

If they were at all curious how her new client knew where she lived, neither Emily nor Katelyn was particularly vocal about that detail, only pleasantly remorseful over parting ways sooner than expected. Hugs and reassurances that she was fine, and Reyes would deposit her on his own way home, Summer made it clear that she was willing to leave with him, damning herself by discarding their concerns.

Having sealed her fate, she allowed herself to be led away with an arm hooked under Reyes' bicep. His strength, his body, searing hers in every place that their skin touched. Perhaps that could be the new source of blame as to why she was utterly losing her mind, the way she had just let herself succumb to his effects.

Chapter Fourteen

By the time they reached her street, unchanneled antagonism took its toll. Torn between intrigue and ire, Summer wallowed in waves of unease. For the second time in three days Reyes had taken a hard left, something she hadn't seen coming. Was this some sort of twisted governmental game the FBI played with their informants or was he just as messed up as Jerrod?

Unpleasant thoughts occupied her mind as they approached her building. She couldn't stop the disturbing comparisons to her ex, even when her gut wanted to disagree. As usual, Reyes, tuned into her turmoil, purposefully made the transition into her house stupidly smooth with little opportunity to argue, let alone talk.

But she wanted the battle, considered it a way to release the volatility swirling inside her. Pride alone held her tongue through the pedestrian flow, just long enough to get up the stairs and inside lest neighbors have another earful of their relationship in action.

"This is the second time you've decided the party's over for me. It would be nice," she gritted out with a modicum of stability once the door was safely closed and they were in private, "if you would catch me up on what your expectations are when I'm in the field or not. Tonight was *my* time, not a mission or a job to deliver on."

"A party, huh?" he asked. "That's what you term your previous evening with Metzinger?"

"You know what I mean."

"Enlighten me, Summer. Let's say I don't know what you mean. And by the way, it was your beautiful eyes that almost begged me to take you home. Should I think this is fun for you? Should I think you view it as a game?"

All her pent-up wrath and tension spewed out. "Are you kidding? Of course this isn't a fun game! You've made me into a liar. You've made me a traitor. You've made me question everything I've done. And yeah, I admit I needed a hand talking my way around it with Katelyn, cause my brain can't think straight. But I'm not a vindictive cheat. I'm not a liar and I don't want to keep feeling like this, do you fucking get that?"

Her volume was erratic, raging all the malevolence the past few weeks had built up. And the evolution of some truly nasty, conflicted confusion.

"Yeah, I do get it," he answered softly in stark contrast to her outburst, which only served to make her angrier. "I do understand."

"Understand what exactly?"

"What it feels likes to be forced into becoming something you're not, regardless of the reasons why."

"No offense, but you have no idea what I'm going through."

"Don't I? I'm here too, going through it all with you but I can't understand what you don't tell me."

"And why should I tell you anything?"

"To help you deal with this better. It's not an easy task we've forced on you."

She let out a clipped, humorless laugh. "You've got

that right. It's not easy. But to be clear, I can handle it."

When she quit prowling around the room, he began his own circling, stopping only once he was directly in front of her, all indications that the game had evolved. "Ms. Halley, with your willpower, I have no doubt. That doesn't mean you can't lean on me a little, help take the edge off. Release some stress." His eyes flared, revealing the edge of something far less altruistic. "Isn't that what you wanted? Why you allowed me to escort you home? Why you haven't kicked me out now that we're here?"

Inches were lost as the ground crumbled beneath her feet. Her intentions, if they ever were guarded, lay exposed between them.

"Exactly," he supplied when she didn't respond. "You haven't told me to leave because you don't want to. You haven't because you aren't going to."

Locking her in his gaze, he waited, then growled, "Tell me, Summer. Tell me you don't want this, and I'll go."

She couldn't. Couldn't say those words, couldn't add yet another lie on top of the dark pile of deceit already corroding her soul. No matter how wrong this all was. No matter his role, or hers. Because what her head wanted, what her fragmented heart sought, betrayed all reason.

When she still didn't speak, his next words grew even more desperate as he came to her, "Please, tell me you don't want me to touch you." A hand slid into her hair, cradling her skull before entwining strands around fingers that flexed with tension. "Please," he said lowly, his breath feathering her cheeks. "Stop me."

She could do no such thing. Instead, she trailed her hand up his arm to where it stroked the back of her head, urging him on in silent plea. On a broken groan, his mouth captured hers in a scorching fusion of lips and tongues and sent her burning beyond thought, riding on the blistering heat with little regard for anything else.

What had simmered from the beginning, what both had gone to great lengths to deny or deflect with cleverly crafted sarcasm and outright distrust, lit into an all-consuming flame.

Summer let it take her down, drowning as his movements became more hurried. He tugged down her jeans, stripping away all pretenses while his mouth never left hers.

Pausing only to slide on a condom, there was no slowing their rhythm as he thrust into her with a frenzied intensity, her passion eliciting a true match.

The orgasm shook her to the core as he simultaneously trembled with his own release. Even though she knew it was dangerous, even though there was no turning back, she was far from sated. She wanted more of him, more of the heat, more of everything…And when they joined again, slower, sweeter, that replete craving was scarcely abated.

Once they made it to her bed, it didn't take long before she slid into sleep with Reyes stretched out at her side. If his presence provided easy comfort after the torrid storm they'd brewed, she told herself it was just the aftermath.

And then, somewhere close to the waking hours of dawn, she dreamed of Keira. Her mind recreated a toddler, healthy, vibrant, and joyfully innocent. And very much alive. There was nothing in the dream child's appearance that resembled Jerrod, as Keira toddled through gauzy grass. Her brain had manifested what her heart felt, which was that she had been the sole parent to her angel baby.

But as the manifestation progressed, numerous, shifting images overlaid pigments on top of one another until all of the background became stripped away. She saw herself now, cleared from beneath the filters, standing in the empty white void, holding Keira's hand while someone else walked toward them.

Someone smiling, someone familiar.

Liam took Keira's other tiny hand in his, while looking down at her like she was the most treasured thing in his life—not something broken.

Then, like ashes in the wind, the disjointed picture was blown apart as consciousness sank ruthless claws into her chest. Heart pounding, her body tightened like a bow and her breathing spasmed. Painfully aware that she wasn't alone like she always was when dreams plagued her, she addressed her physical reaction with brutal concentration. With each uneven breath, she relaxed coiled tendons, loosened bones, smoothed out joints, until finally her lungs settled.

Quelling the calamity one stretch at a time, she lay in supine tree pose for an extended period, seeking balance, intentionally regaining control.

It was only once she lowered both legs that she realized Reyes was lying on his side, fully awake and watching her. "Everything okay?"

"Mmhmm," she murmured, fearful of speaking actual words.

Then she jolted back, realizing with horror that as he reached up and drew his fingertips across her cheek, they came away damp. The tears betrayed her without her even opening her mouth. Summer had assumed they had dried enough to be overlooked. Clearly, she was wrong. Lately, though, dreams of Keira left her sad but not crying. This one had packed a harsher punch.

And he kept right on watching her with enduring patience, an evolved expectancy that their intimacy might elicit more honest disclosure.

Through a melancholy wave of numbness, she swiped at her cheeks and leveled her voice as best she could, "Just a bad dream, I'm fine." Without waiting to see if that answer satisfied, Summer tossed back the blanket and headed for the bathroom, yanking the hot water on full blast.

Part of her was relieved while another part remained disappointed when he didn't join her. The fact that he stayed away confirmed the bad dream comment didn't suffice. But she refused to plunge headfirst into stupidity, it would only lead to her getting hurt and she wasn't sure that the tangled mass of her heart could handle any more blows.

He had exited the bed while she'd been in the shower so once alone and dressed, Summer went in search of food.

And found Reyes in front of the stove once more. Processing the déjà vu sensation, she brewed coffee in silence while he took care of the eggs. What should have struck her as pretentious and assuming, taking it upon himself to make breakfast again, lacked true impact. Had they really developed some sort of routine after so little time? In all the ways they challenged each other, these moments were oddly simple.

When his gaze met hers, she didn't hide the spreading smile. Indeed, now that she had compartmentalized certain emotions, she was alert enough to openly drink in the sight before her. All six plus feet of Liam Reyes stood barefoot in her kitchen. Loose, drawstring shorts hung low on his hips, accentuating his carved form. He'd donned a T-shirt; the soft cotton directly contrasted with the lean yet substantial muscles that delineated his arms—all of which reminded her she needed to discover where he kept extra clothes and other sorts of miscellaneous basics.

Seeing him undone and barefoot stirred a myriad of reactions—most significantly, the fact that she wanted to have sex with him again. Now.

This she could manage. This she could handle.

Approaching the stove, she made her immediacy obvious as she slid a hand along his thigh, causing a stilling of movement. He looked down at where her fingers gripped and flexed against the fabric, watched as they perused closer to pulsing heat already blooming to life beneath her palm. It caused her own blood to heat her core, responding to his pulse with a heartbeat of its own.

Shooting her a searing side eye, with a flick of the wrist, he swiftly shut off the burner and grabbed hold of her hips while spinning her around to have those bones brushing up against the counter.

With a gentleness that was in stark contrast to the urgent demand gliding between her thighs from behind, he took her hands up over her head, laying them flat against the upper cabinet before he wrapped one around her wrist and gripped the other at her hipbone, creating a buffer against the edge of the counter, all while sweeping soft, shivery kisses up and down the column of her neck. Shifting aside her shorts, he pushed into her, slowly at first, both relishing the torturous slide. But the gentleness he used to hold her quickly evolved into a hushed ferocity which left them both panting for breath.

The food was cold by the time they reached the table but by then it hardly mattered because her appetite was suddenly ravenous.

Once they had finished eating, over steaming mugs of coffee, Summer couldn't help but cling to an unresolved point of contention from the night before. It was still a safer path, considering where her heart wanted to lead her, so she took the cowardly way out.

"Are you bothered by the fact that you played a role in deceiving my family?"

Surprise flickered a bit, but then he leaned back in the chair, languid limbs, coffee in hand, causally studying her. "Deceit is part of the game I'm required to play. And that dishonesty is utilized to catch bad guys."

He might make it sound simple, but she'd come to suspect that was also a strategy for him. As soon as someone underestimates the deception, the other can strike with the advantage. "Including me."

"Does it?" When she raised an eyebrow, he qualified, "Yes, I've been fairly transparent about the amount of dirt we gathered on you. It's how this works and it went a long way towards making our offer appear non-negotiable. But there are still things we don't know. That I don't know."

Defenses rose in a kneejerk response and couldn't be stopped. While gulping coffee, she set her expression into a straight line. He couldn't make her talk, no matter how well he fucked her. For those moments when they were together, it felt like she wouldn't fall into a million jagged pieces.

That didn't mean she was struck stupid.

Though it cost her, Summer casually raised a shoulder. "True enough. Just as there are things I don't know about this investigation, there are plenty of things I don't know about you."

"What you don't know is critical, both for the success of the operation as well as for your protection. If, for some reason Metzinger makes you, the less you know, the better."

They actually thought Jerrod was capable of extracting information from her, through force if necessary. After absorbing this bit of rationale, she voiced her doubts. "Jerrod has done a lot of things for which he needs to be held accountable. But purposefully hurting me to gain information? I don't know about that one…"

"Even now you hesitate, that's a smart thing," he said. "You never know what someone is capable of until their backs are up against a wall and they're out of options."

"Fair point. And by the way, it didn't pass over me, the fact that you said it's a game for you."

"Never thought it did, Summer. Fair point as well," he acknowledged.

By acknowledging it—rather than refuting the claim—a natural suspension divided the conversation as both slipped into mutual contemplation. So, when he rose a few moments later to come trace her jawline with his thumb, ending with a possessive kiss that defied the context of their situation, she felt even more flummoxed as her instincts fought against one another, over logic, over reason. He was playing her too, even if she could inexplicably claim that the desire and the compassion he'd shown her felt genuine. A hardened piece of her soul chastised all the bruised soft parts, telling herself it was for the best if he kept on being her buffer with the other agents, because how long would that last once all the nasty details of the truth finally emerged? That was the real possibility, the one that kept her awake at night, the one that haunted her every time one of those threatening texts illuminated her screen.

She could ask more questions; she could push harder to discover more about the case against Jerrod. But she suspected Reyes' shield worked both ways.

At the transparent question in his eyes, Summer pulled away from his touch, using the dirty dishes as an excuse to walk away from his steady appraisal. Without rejoining him at the table once the task was finished, she spoke to the air as she kept walking toward the bedroom, cementing the avoidance. "I have to get ready for work."

Her movements stayed methodical, one step in front of the other, no room for overthinking, for brooding, on all the things that couldn't be changed. When enough time had passed that she assumed he had done one of those vanishing acts of his and disappeared out of the house, she slipped back out of her room, only to be greeted with a jab of dismay when Reyes appeared right where she'd left him.

He made a move like he wanted to approach her again, touch her again, which had her tightening her arms across her chest to make it clear she didn't want the contact.

He stopped, stayed where he was. "What's wrong?"

He shouldn't be here, he shouldn't care. His concern worked just as impactfully as the physical contact she did not want. Shoulders stiff, she remained where she was, creating a standoff. "Nothing."

"Summer…what happened between us, that stays outside the investigation, I—"

She had to stop him before he said anything to make it that much harder. Woodenly, she adjusted her shoulders before casting her gaze to the window, unable to look at him. She coated her voice in disinterest. "I simply prefer to be wanted. By choice. No harm, no foul, though."

She could have sworn he murmured her name once, so softly the fragile note barely made it to her ears. This time, when she glanced back to face him, she didn't back down.

When he didn't deny what she'd said, she departed for Longtime Sun without a single look back. With a hardened heart, she was determined to focus on her clients and leave Liam Reyes far, far behind.

Chapter Fifteen

Katelyn waited until Summer was halfway through her appointments before showing up to grill her. Rounding the corner heading out of the treatment area, Summer drew up short when she saw her sister conversing with Ayana in covertly hushed tones.

Whether they purposefully put on the mock whispers or were being courteous to those deep into their acu-naps, she appreciated they weren't disturbing anyone, save her. It didn't take a genius to infer the topic of conversation. And if Ayana couldn't figure out who "Liam the client" was, she was playing it off quite well.

Katelyn smiled broadly. "Hey, Summer."

Instead of acknowledging her, Summer crisply addressed her employee, "Ayana, those sheets should be ready to go in the dryer, if you could check them, please."

Clearly getting the hint, Ayana exchanged an equally big grin with her sister before heading toward the back.

"So, correct me if I'm wrong," Katelyn began, "because last time we talked, you were talking to Jerrod, *entertaining* whatever possibilities. And yet, tall, dark and handsome shows up to help you home last night. Did you plan that one in advance?"

"Certainly not," Summer retorted with more resolve than she actually felt. If she could just hang on to indignancy over the implication that she'd sleep around with multiple men—and enjoy it—she wouldn't risk breaking down. "As he said, he's a client who just happened to be out where we were. A coincidence only. Nothing planned."

Katelyn raised one disbelieving brow. Fine, she didn't need her sister to believe her. But as stubbornness kicked in, Summer remembered how imperative it was for her family to believe it, for the sake of her future and the case. "I'm telling you, Katelyn, I'm not involved with Liam. He is just a client."

"Client or not, he's a total smoke show. And a fantastic opportunity to give Jerrod a taste of his own medicine."

"Jerrod never cheated on me," she asserted as heat rose in her cheeks out of frustration over being manipulated into saying something that held no merit.

"So, you are into him then," Katelyn concluded. "Trust me, who could blame you? And just because your husband never physically betrayed you, doesn't mean he didn't engage in other kinds of betrayal."

Summer didn't know which statement to counter first. "I'm not getting into this right now. Where's Mom? What are you up to today? Want to get a treatment?"

"A treatment sounds good, but it'll have to be another time. Mom's at the house with Gabe while I run a few errands."

Errands that apparently included checking up on her, Summer thought. But if her sister was out and about, that could only mean good things health-wise. "Okay. Well, enjoy your day with her and let me know if you have a change of plans before she heads home and we can figure something out."

"I know when I'm getting dismissed." Katelyn slapped a hand to her chest in mock offense. "But before I accept your dismissal and go let Mom know you're healthy, sound and all in one piece, I want to ask you something."

Summer couldn't help the influx of anxiety as she waited for her sister to continue. Long ingrained habits always seemed to creep back up no matter how valiant her efforts to change. It didn't always have to be about cancer or money. "Yeah?" she asked cautiously.

"It's more a decision, I guess, than a question. I'd like to take you up on your work offer. Gabe and I talked about it and we both think it might be a good thing for us, for me."

She tried not to let the surprise show because it should have made her happy that Katelyn felt well enough to work. Yet, unwanted apprehension kept pressing into her consciousness. It *was* about money, of sorts. Only this seemed like too seamless of an agreement—especially after she'd seen the truth of her offer etch disappointment across Katelyn's face the week earlier.

Before Summer could ask why now, why the sudden change of heart, Ayana reappeared. "Sheets and the latest herbal shipment are taken care of and it looks like the next appointment's in five."

"Thanks, Ayana. Katelyn, I need to get back to the treatment room, I can call you later so we can figure out how you want to do this, like with hours and training."

"Sounds good," she said, sending her a relieved smiled. "I knew you'd help me out."

That struck another hard chord as Summer watched Katelyn leave, wondering over the swell of nerves when it was all she'd had to offer her sister in the first place.

Katelyn had claimed she understood when the money stopped coming after Summer disclosed the loss of the baby and impending divorce, but Summer could never erase the devastation that altered her sister's face after she dropped that news.

Not sorrow, not mere sympathy for the miscarriage and breakup. No, there had been clear, visible despair, and it had festered inside Summer, causing existing dark water to grow even murkier. She didn't *want* to think these things, face these inconsistencies…not with family, who were always supposed to have her back.

"Summer, hey," Ayana's words drew her out of those revolving thoughts. "You've got a timer going off and Jen walking toward the door. You okay?"

"Yeah sorry, I'll go wake up Mr. Bradley if you could get the next client settled? She knows the drill."

"Sure thing." The girl turned to leave, then stopped again. "Did I hear right, is Katelyn going to work here now?"

"Yes, it seems that way."

"That'll be awesome! Keeping with family. Love it," she said before moving to greet and check in the client.

Speculating over why she didn't feel the same, Summer tried grasping a fraction of Ayana's sentiments. Yes, they were keeping it all in the family, without the secrecy, without any games. Yet it felt like she'd just stumbled into another scenario where she ended up losing more than she bargained for.

****

The following night, Summer sat in the silence of Jerrod's kitchen, an untouched plate of charcuterie and fruit at her elbow. A glass of wine sat undisturbed on the wide expanse of quartz.

She'd just let Reyes into the house—proceeding with business as usual—when Jerrod texted, asking for assistance with an undisclosed matter. While *she* had wanted to ignore it, Reyes insisted she not only respond but agree to go within the hour.

She wasn't ready to face Jerrod, wasn't ready to act like everything was okay. She felt scraped open and raw, and hoped Reyes would let her stay home. With him. But there was a job to get done, he reminded her. If feeling used and so easily sent away hurt, it was her own doing.

She hadn't been forced to sleep with him. No, she'd done that all of her own free will, even if their coming together was probably inevitable. The heady friction they'd sparked off each other flamed bright enough to engulf her entire soul.

If she was being truthful with herself, she had never been with anyone who could make her burn quite that way. Not even Jerrod, who once knew how to light up all those parts of her—and quite well.

Despite the traitorous side that fantasized about seducing Reyes again, he'd been uncharacteristically urgent, impressing on her how critical it was to the operation and the bureau that she produce tangible results. It was rare to see such a spike in the immediacy communicated without his typical amount of poise.

Arguing was futile.

So here she sat, alone and waiting for her ex-husband, ensconced again within walls that spoke of horrible acts, witness to all the shortcomings, all the deceit. Just like her own home, purchased with tainted funds, as though she were just as much a criminal as those she sought to take down.

Unable to eat Jerrod's food or drink his wine, considering them attempts to coerce her with expensive tastes and dark reminders of who had helped pay her way. But if she couldn't choke down his bribes, the thing she *had* to do was be the character they all needed her to portray and eventually, Jerrod might reveal his next move. It took a while, but when he finally reemerged from an interior section of the house, he didn't come alone.

Cameron filed in behind him. Gripping her hands together against the skittering of her pulse, she willed herself to stay steady and intentionally softened the hold. Thinking about Reyes and everything that needed to be done, she reminded herself that this fight was for her freedom too, not just to end something that should have been stopped a long time ago.

"Cameron," she acknowledged in a hard-won neutral tone.

"Well, hey, Summer. Long time no see."

Instead of responding to his obtuseness, she turned her gaze to Jerrod. "This is kind of last minute and I don't have that much time." She had to play at least slightly annoyed at the lack of notice or risk earning more suspicion. "What do you need?"

"Thanks for coming," he replied silkily, reaching for her hand, pressing a kiss against knuckles that still needed to regain some blood flow.

Fighting the urge to snatch her hand away, Summer watched as he held on a bit longer, purposefully lingering his lips on her skin and watching her expression in return. Always testing, always measuring.

Summer sent him a smile that she prayed looked put

out yet flattered. When he withdrew his mouth, Jerrod resumed a stance beside Cameron, attesting to a sense of solidarity. Could she adopt the same guise? They were supposed to be on the same crooked side, the same one from which she had willfully ostracized herself. But here she sat with a proverbial noose around her neck, one that could be yanked up at any moment by a very intimidating government entity.

Stay in the moment, stop thinking so much. As far as mantras went, it was mediocre.

Then Jerrod started talking, forcing her attention back to the present. "After your recent assistance, Cameron mentioned you were intrigued in learning more about our latest interests."

Damn it. She'd assumed Cameron wouldn't stay quiet but knowing it and facing it were two different things. "I wouldn't say intrigued—" she blurted before cutting the sentence off with a nip of teeth. Pivoting quickly, she smiled again. "What new interests? Are you referring specifically to what I assisted Cameron in retrieving the other day?"

"Yes, that one specifically." If Jerrod noticed the tone shift or was irritated with being cut off, he showed no reaction. "Although, of course there have been many others. We've had a lot of growth since you've been gone. Expanding, branching out, altering acquisitions…"

Her senses began to tingle. Here was the exact type of dirt her orchestrators sought. The very thing that made her equally nervous.

"Hot items still intact are easy to trace, even though our crew is slick at covering tracks," Cameron interjected.

"We did well," she agreed easily—because it was true. They were good at what they did.

"But things started getting more slippery than usual," Jerrod continued. "Several of our regular contacts began asking too many questions, making the actual goods harder to move."

Reyes had told her the FBI had successfully intercepted a few of his associates. Maybe they weren't so far off from snagging Jerrod after all.

"So, as you know, sitting on stolen merch for too long creates more liability, more opportunity for failure. And since you asked, we thought we'd bring you in on our current project." Jerrod turned to the backpack Summer had not realized was sitting behind him and withdraw an odd-shaped piece of metal the approximate size of a loaf of bread.

Turning it over his hands a few times, her ex demonstrated a carefulness with the object that from first impression did not seem warranted. Yet he held it as though it possessed immense value. "Do you know what this is, Summer?"

"No." She shook her head, fighting the urge to double check the monitoring app. They could hear him, they knew where she was so it should be all good. Despite knowing her safety wasn't at immediate risk, it didn't stop the shriek of instincts that warned her it could change in an instant.

"This is a catalytic converter."

She laughed a little when he didn't elaborate. "Sorry, you say that like it means something to me."

"This baby makes us a lot of bank," Cameron said, stepping in and taking the converter from his boss while exercising the same level of care in handling it, thus reinforcing its worth.

A warning flash flared in Jerrod's eyes, but Cameron was oblivious. Clearly, he didn't know him as well as Summer did, since bragging tended to get people gone in this line of work. "We pluck these bad boys out of the exhaust system, extract the goods and move it on. Much harder to follow."

"What goods?" she asked. "It looks like just another piece of the engine."

"The purpose of the converter is to reduce emissions from a vehicle's exhaust," Jerrod spoke in a voice gone dangerously soft. "To do that, precious metals are used to filter them out."

Of cars, she knew little. She didn't think Jerrod knew all that much, but when he made up his mind to do something, she had no doubt he would learn whatever was needed in order to succeed. "Okay," she drew out the syllable, struggling to understand the point. Then it dawned on her—they removed the metals, not actually selling the converter itself. "So, you take out the precious metals, that's where the value is."

Jerrod sent her a brief nod of approval. "That's right. Once removed from the converter, untraceable precious metals like platinum and rhodium are easily hidden and easily transported. Meaning better outcomes for us."

"And you know who gets all that beautiful, expensive metal out to be outsourced? This guy." Cameron, not wising up, thrust a thumb back at his chest.

No longer able to temper his irritation, Jerrod motioned to Cameron, who in turn threw up his hands like he was innocent. "What? You're the one who wanted her here. Said that she should be brought up to speed."

"That doesn't mean discretion isn't advantageous."

"I don't get it, bro. Either you let the bitch back in or she stays out. Permanently. If you want my opinion—"

"If I wanted your opinion," Jerrod sneered, "I'd have enlisted you for more than just your sleight of hand."

Cameron scowled, temper overtaking arrogance. "There should be no in between with what she knows. I'm not trying to get taken down because your wifey can't make up her mind. And since when did you turn all soft? Is it when she stopped letting you hit that sweet—"

Jerrod's fist flew fast, smashing down onto the island and silencing Cameron who in turn shot Summer a dark look. "On that, my friend, we can both agree. There will be no in between…"

A jerk of his head followed before Jerrod stalked out, Cameron trailing behind, which left Summer standing alone in the kitchen. Their exit couldn't have come at a better time. Cameron's stupidity was her opportunity and, seizing it, she pecked out a fast text before she could be detected, making sure Reyes had gotten the earful about the converters.

A split second went by before he responded.

—*get out—now—*

She took that to mean he'd heard the important stuff.

Mentally grasping for a valid reason to escape— using her sister again did not seem smart—Summer rearranged the food on the plate then hastily dumped her wine down the drain.

Just as she was setting the glass back down, a plausible excuse still evading her, Jerrod reappeared, slinking up behind her and wrapping his arms around her waist. She held motionless, heart pounding, wondering if he'd seen her messing with the hors d'oeuvres and pouring out the expensive alcohol. Could he hear the beat of her blood pumping madly against his chest? Did it betray her, or would he assume it was stemming from anticipation?

"Cameron can't hold his tongue. Although," he purred as he turned her to face him. "Lately, neither can I."

Like a promise, that tongue was now violating her skin, intruding into her mouth and demanding an answer to an unresolved query. Less of a query, really. More of a horrifying declaration.

Releasing her when she didn't respond, he whipped her around, roughly pushing her back against the counter and digging his fingers into her flesh while the cold stone bit into her pelvis. In an unnervingly similar position to how Reyes had taken her in her own kitchen, this advance lacked any amount of care and consideration.

"Wish we could finish what we started," he breathed against her neck as he pulled her hand down and wrapped it around his cock, making her grip him through the fabric of his pants. "But I've got to deal with this fucker. You could always come back later, stay over."

Desperate for distance, Summer ventured, "I'm not trying to come between you and Cameron. He's one of the best you have."

"That may be true, but I don't tolerate disrespect. The only reason his mouth hasn't landed him in worse shit is because his finesse is invaluable. But I *always* call the shots, you know that and so does he. Unfortunately, reminders are sometimes necessary."

Even though they were still fully clothed, she was

overwhelmed by a ridiculous sense of betrayal as the pressure beneath her palm increased. This was a job.

Reyes had a job—she *was* that job.

The cold, brutal truth of it kept her hands relatively steady as his hand held hers tightly to his erection. Revulsion was a steady drum, ever present. When he moved her hand back and forth down the shaft, vile sensory overload jeopardized her steadiness.

This was *her* reminder. Maybe Jerrod wouldn't let her go after all and she would be forced to have sex with her ex-husband so shortly after being consumed by another man. Consumed like a hot, wanton flame.

She could admit that Reyes had awakened a desire that had long gone dormant inside of her. A passionate fire that rode on private, intimate pleasure, the rush of feeling only achieved from taking an equally matched lover. And not just any lover. She'd learned after a very short, experimental period of promiscuity that it wasn't sex with anyone that would satisfy, it was sex with the right ones. The ones who relished and fed her drive. The ones who understood and cherished those sides of her.

Despite the level of recklessness, despite the need to deny, Reyes made her feel all those things. Cherished. Understood. Accepted. Of all the people she could have tangled with, Reyes was the one who had roused and matched that fire.

"So, is that a yes?"

He'd asked a question—and she'd failed to answer correctly. She'd also failed in following Reyes' command to get out. Trapped now, because there was only one way he'd let her go. Hating herself for doing what needed to be done, she kept her hand firm against his cock. "Yes, Jerrod, I'll come back."

"Perfect," he murmured with smug satisfaction. "Answer your phone."

Releasing her, he strode away, presumably to go set Cameron straight.

And she beat her retreat as fast as she could, running headlong into the night and back to Reyes. Back to safety.

Chapter Sixteen

It was through a clenched jaw, in which her supposedly levelheaded babysitter addressed her when she blasted through her front door. Perched on a chair, not really sitting yet not really standing, Reyes' body was positioned like a panther ready to pounce. She wished it didn't look quite so enticing.

"You took longer."

When their eyes collided, she knew he'd heard what Jerrod had asked her. Knew he'd heard her subsequent agreement to return later.

"Sorry," she snapped with a considerable amount of malice. "I can't just walk in and out of there as I please. Or do anything without a fucking monitor to point out everything wrong about it."

"Ditto."

The pithy response further triggered her indignance. "Again, I must remind you, this is *not* my choice."

Whatever line they had crossed together seemed to have redrawn itself, placing each back on opposing sides.

"And I must remind you, Summer, that it is entirely your choice. Beginning all the way back from when you decided to take up with your *husband* in his criminal enterprises."

She negated this comment with a terse head shake. "How can you throw that in my face? I know what I did, which is why I'm standing here being reprimanded by you. It's why I stood between Cameron and Jerrod earlier, letting my *ex* defend an honor I no longer have to offer. Maybe this doesn't matter to you or anyone else, but I swear to God I would do anything for my sister. Even pay this price."

His level of alertness magnified tenfold. "What, precisely, does Katelyn have to do with Metzinger's stunts?"

Immediately, she realized the slip. They stared each other down, neither giving the other an inch. And then, her guilt snapped. "She has absolutely everything to do with this."

It felt like an explosion, the rash of resentment and pain finally bursting free. "Her cancer diagnosis has everything to do with this. All the way down to the last penny I laundered so she could keep her accounts paid in full."

In a rare moment of naked disconcertment, Reyes looked at her, causing her to feel freshly vulnerable and exposed. Apparently, he didn't know the rest. She hadn't been completely sure, the uncertainty playing endless games inside her head of whether or when he was simply waiting for the right time to leverage her sins.

"You were paying her medical bills?"

"That's right. And kept doing so right up until…" Trailing off, Summer clamped her lips together. It was bad enough that she had just admitted to laundering money in order to deal with Katelyn's bills, she wouldn't make it worse by talking about Keira too.

"Until?"

"Until I couldn't take it anymore. And she had reached another remission by then. But now even that's shot to shit again," she added under her breath, less for his benefit, but he homed right in on it anyway.

"What do you mean?"

"I mean, her cancer's active again," she said on a wary sigh. "We found out a few weeks ago. Or at least, that's when she told me."

"When you reluctantly answered her call out back."

The man missed nothing.

"Yes. She finally came clean with the fact that her doctor changed the chemotherapy plan. It had slowed the tumor growth but not fully prevented its return."

His face clouded with sympathy, reducing most of its earlier tension. But she didn't want it, didn't know how to accept it, when she held so much responsibility, so much blame, in her own dirty hands. Needing to shift the tone, she pushed forward, "I know this means I can face more charges, me admitting to money laundering because I know your duty is to the bureau…"

"Fuck the bureau."

"Reyes," she started, then amended it to a quiet "Liam" when he shot her a divisive look. "I'm fairly sure you don't mean that," she added on in a whisper, suddenly nervous someone else could be listening on her phone, even though she'd cleared the app out as soon as she was through the door.

"At the moment, yeah, I do. At the moment, I'm less worried about new charges being brought and more concerned with how to get the FBI to grant full immunity, especially in light of these new details."

"I sincerely doubt they care very much as to why I broke the law." Then, slowly it occurred to her what he'd actually said. "I thought I *was* being offered immunity."

On a growl, he whirled around to stalk over to the window, then back. The ridges in his facial muscles deepened again, their steely quality revealing a startling fury that struggled to be restrained. She wondered how deep his anger ran as well as all the sources it stemmed from. "That's what they claim as they wield their power and control. If they didn't make you think that—if I hadn't made you think you'd get it—then you would never have agreed to this."

"So as of now, my fate is still to be determined."

"I'm sorry."

The impact of his admission sank in with brutal, breath stealing swiftness. No matter what she did, no matter how high she jumped when they called for it—a heartless government entity with no qualms about crushing her was still in full control of her destiny.

She swallowed the harsh lump in her throat. "This puts you in a difficult position, so I'm sorry too."

She couldn't believe she'd voiced her regrets for him, but it was true as well. She'd just unleashed a damning admission, and it hadn't been on purpose. If she had just been able to keep the laundering under wraps, it would've been the best for everyone involved.

When he walked to her, gaze intent but slightly softened, she fought against the unnerving urge to seek him out for comfort. It would be easy to slide forward and take the things he'd offered. She could stop denying herself, but at what cost?

Always aware, he came no closer than the distance it took to lightly cup her elbows, giving them a gentle bend. It was a mild grasp, allowing her to easily pull back if she chose. Torn, she stayed where she was, allowing his hands to remain on her, yet moving no closer. It amazed her how considerate he could be when it was just the two of them. Except there was never just the two of them to consider.

"There is nothing to apologize for. Why don't you think of us as having a confidentiality clause moving forward and whatever you share with me—for the benefit of the operation. I'm obligated to keep it between us in order to better support you. That is what they assigned me for, ultimately," he continued when she arched a skeptical brow. "Yes, I am to surveil you but also ensure your full participation. This is an additional caveat—your full participation rests on my silence in this matter."

Sucking in a breath, Summer felt the magnetic pull tighten, inciting her forward. Resisting, she shifted her shoulder blades, "For a lot of reasons, that sounds too good to believe. Considering…well, everything."

"I get it."

Taking her cue, he dropped her elbow but not before sweeping a thumb along the sensitive underside, resulting in the remembrance of the insidious promise of going back to Jerrod tonight. Now that she was home, home with Reyes, the thought made her so physically ill, her stomach coiled into nasty, mutinous knots. Battling the nausea, hating how weak her voice sounded as she implored, "Please, I can't go back there tonight. I know what he'll try to do and if I go back, I'll have to let him. Don't make me."

She wouldn't beg, but it was coming close to necessary when he didn't respond for what seemed like an eternity even as a storm rebloomed in his eyes, swirling and tumultuous. When he remained quiet, she reiterated her plea, this time with more conviction, "Liam, please."

That appeared to snap the hold over his self-control

and this time, she didn't resist the pressure winding between them and his swift, reclaiming grip that was no longer soft. Expelling a pent-up breath, he growled lowly beside her neck, "I have no right to do this with you" right before proceeding to capture her mouth.

Voraciously alive, they took from each other, both giving in return. If this was how it felt to forget for a while, to be entirely lost in him, swept away on their living, beating connection, she determined it might be worth whatever sacrifice was demanded.

The more they gave, the more she sought until it wasn't enough. She maneuvered him toward the couch before dropping to kneel before him. He watched with such blatant intensity as she pulled the length of him free and as soon as her mouth made contact, the sounds he groaned out fed her ravenous, consuming hunger.

When his movements turned unsteady and he roughly threaded his fingers into her hair while grinding out her name, she rose, shifting him down onto the couch to climb on top, taking him in and riding them both the rest of the way over the sharp, greedy edge.

Afterward, she slid down beside him, entwining limbs and fitting themselves into a spoon. For a few long beats, their equally elevated heart rates occupied her attention. Their bodies felt melded together, synced, even after he had pulled out.

Dangerous notions swirled in her head. It felt too good to lie here, afterglow cliché be damned. She wasn't so far in denial as to claim that what they had together was average or ordinary. Perhaps accepting that truth would help her get less hurt in the end. If only.

I prefer to be wanted.

Her own words came back to haunt her except there

was no longer a way to discern where her want ended and his began and she let herself revel in the secret idea of them for a few stolen moments.

It killed her when she knew she had to ask the next thing, breaking apart the refuge built on illusion. "Do you think your colleagues will be satisfied with learning Jerrod is targeting catalytic converters?"

The question sounded as disheartened as she felt. But this is why she could never forget that it was never just about the two of them, whatever it was they were doing together, because there would always be those other, unprecedented factors.

A challenge against those demands, in a casually intimate way, he slowly traced a finger across her hip tattoo, following the lines of the inked dandelion flower sending seeds trailing up her torso. "It's important intel, Summer. I will let Jenkins know what you've found out."

"Jenkins?"

"The special agent in charge of this task force. My boss."

She almost twisted around to look at him but was suddenly wary of what she might see there. Recalling what he'd said against her cheek right before the embrace had spiraled into something more, she considered what he must be thinking once again.

It was wrong what was happening between them. He knew it and so did she.

If the FBI found out, retribution was an active fear, and not just for her. But even if she wanted to talk about what this would mean for them if someone were to learn the truth, there was little question that he was already well aware of the repercussions. She registered that fact along with the resignation that his hand had stopped caressing her skin.

"You sort of sound how I do whenever I talk about Cameron. I take it it's not such a... positive dynamic between you two?"

"Huh," he supplied without explanation, indicating it was beyond her realm of business to ask, which was beyond irritating. Whoever Jenkins was, he clearly held stock in her fate, if not the ability to dictate the entire fucking outcome.

"You didn't seem quite as disturbed about seeing Cameron this time." He sidestepped the issue casually, even though she knew there was nothing casual about the observance.

"I thought of you and knew what needed to be done."

She sensed his smile returning as he settled more snugly against her back and resumed the stroking motion across her hip. Although it wasn't always obvious through the arrogance he wore like a second skin, he rarely showed genuine calm or easiness, which made his contentment now all the more satisfying.

"That sounds like a great exercise in compartmentalizing. But even though you got a good result, it's okay to say otherwise. I told you I would help you through this."

Here again were expectations being thrown at her feet, asking that she drop her guard after they'd been together. Wasn't knowing about Katelyn, about the laundering, enough? Her reasons had been laid bare, stripping away some layers but transparency was still out of reach.

Squeezing her eyes shut, Summer wished for the strength to own her full truth.

The decision—if she were to make one—was taken out of her hands when his phone's incoming alerts began to incessantly pierce the air. "Fuck," he muttered, easing out from behind her.

So lovely and naked, she watched him stride across the room, grabbing up his pants as he moved. When he disappeared from view, she knew it would take a while before he would come back to her—in many ways.

No matter what he told her about being on her side, when he switched back to agent mode, Summer didn't delude herself into thinking that he could keep her entirely out of the assignment category. Or if he even wanted to. It probably helped him work better to consider her in that way. Less bias, more objectivity. And the capability for ruthlessness. He couldn't change his role any more than she could. Yet, their dichotomies seemed to ebb and flow, never permanently attaching to anything clear, anything substantial.

The lack of permanency left Summer to contend with a barrage of incessant thoughts, while all texts from Jerrod remained unread.

****

She asked Ayana to stay an hour after closing so together they could walk Katelyn through the reservation system and the various social media accounts for the business.

In an ideal arrangement, she would prefer for her sister to take over their feeds and tweets entirely as the whole concept irritated her. But business-wise, it was self-sabotaging to not stay present on socials.

"Our app allows people to book slots in real time and then it populates here," Summer explained once Katelyn was settled at the front desk studying the screen

167

with her.

"This part is pretty self-explanatory, but you have to make sure that if someone calls or emails for an appointment instead of using the app that you enter it here as well, so it shows that it's been booked."

"Okay, seems simple enough."

"Nice thing about technology, it makes it simple. The appointment request is then sent to the queue where I can approve or deny it. Ideally, all first timers will book the additional ten-minute consultation slot or at the very least notate on the booking the reason why they are seeking treatment. Again, that's ideal and not always the case, especially if we have openings and I allow time for a walk-in."

"Do you get a lot of them?"

"Walk-ins? No, not commonly, but I want to make the clinic accessible to as many people as possible, which is why I use a sliding pay scale.

"We also use the tablets to track the time in the chairs," she continued. "Some patients like to tell us how long they can rest for, and we can make adjustments for them. Others will stay the full forty-five minutes—and beyond it if they could. The chairs are assigned a position number so that it's not confusing whose time goes with which seat. Which is also why we have to space out our appointment slots, anticipating that someone will want to use the full duration."

"Got it," Katelyn said before stifling a yawn.

Her sister was being uncharacteristically quiet and agreeable, which was worrisome. Mood swings were a part of Katelyn's process though and if Summer didn't want to be grilled about Jerrod, Reyes and the whole mess she was dealing with, it only seemed fair to keep her disquiet to herself.

"We'll have you shadow with Ayana for the first few shifts anyway to make sure you've got the hang of entering all the stuff before I bring you in solo. But seriously, I'm glad you want to work."

"Yeah," Ayana agreed, coming up behind them. "Keeping it in the fam, I love it. Oh, and did she show you my website ideas? I want to design a *much* better one for her, if she'll let me."

"Just her lack of posting, but that's an easy fix."

"Summer needs a little help keeping it fresh for her followers. Well, a lot of help, actually."

"Not surprising. She's pretty socially inept."

"Hey. I'm still standing here," Summer retorted without heat. "I just happen to believe in actually living one's life instead of making a parody out of it so the world can think I'm so much more fabulous than I am."

"See, she's using big words to cover up the fact that she's terrible at coming up with stuff to post."

"Parody, fallacy, whatever ten-dollar word you want to use for making things look unrealistically better than they really are works for me. But this is for work, ladies. No personal stuff. Work only," she repeated before stepping aside to let Ayana take the lead on showing her the necessary housekeeping tasks.

Summer could literally hear eyeballs rolling in sockets without needing to turn back around and catch a glimpse of her sister's reaction. At least she felt well enough for sarcasm.

Staying at the desk to knock out the remaining end-of-day items, she continued to keep an ear open for the two as they moved throughout the treatment area, locating supplies and talking through the steps on how to prepare a chair for a patient. A quick camaraderie appeared to be forming, which instilled confidence in Summer that she'd left Katelyn in capable hands.

With that piece falling into place, she was able to wrap up her to-do list ten minutes earlier than mentally projected. Taking some of the unexpected time to simply sit while she waited for Ayana and Katelyn to finish, Summer was reluctant to pick up her phone when it vibrated beside her. When she did eventually look at it, she knew instantly she should have heeded those instincts. Anxiety bloomed as the burner number read out across the screen.

A division of her brain had been preparing for something to come of the other night. Jerrod would never tolerate being turned down—or blown off. He would figure out a way to punish her, she knew. For her failure to answer, for her refusal to bend to his wishes. She had denied him sex, a reprehensible act in his mind. And was inevitably seeking her out with whatever this was about to turn into.

Summer found her fears confirmed when she read the short, cryptic text. She had five minutes to call the next number provided. Upon a quick glance, she confirmed Katelyn and Ayana were still chatting away in the treatment area, paying her no attention.

Without a word, she slipped out through the back entrance, stepping into the alley running between hers and the next building. Twice she went to hit the phone key. Twice she stopped. Reyes should know before she made the call.

She checked the time and saw that her five minutes were basically already up. Quickly, she placed the call and was greeted by a heavy exhale on the second ring.

"Hello?" she questioned curtly, determined not to let her anxiety be obvious.

A few seconds of hard breathing assaulted her ear before a gravelly, unidentifiable voice spoke. "Your assistance is required."

"I figured. Tell Jerrod I—"

"You will leave your car in your suite's designated client parking," the heavy voice interrupted. "When the lot is clear of your clientele, you will then report the vehicle to Five Star Towing and allow them to come collect it."

"You want me to have my own car towed?" she clarified, now baffled.

"Once the vehicle is impounded, you will go to the lot to pick it up. While you are taking care of the payment and they are retrieving the car, you will alleviate them of their lot key."

"Lot key?" she repeated, struggling to wrap her mind around any of what the rocky voice was relaying.

"Yes. Five Star Towing is one of the few companies here that does not use a high-tech lock on their gate. A basic padlock is all that separates us from the cars. So, they are who you will call."

This was insanity. Weren't there cameras? Everyone had cameras, including her historic building. If someone wanted to dig a little deeper into any kind of footage, it would be obvious that she had parked her own car to then have it towed, which would look beyond suspicious. Success seemed extremely slim.

"Who is this?" Summer snapped at the altered voice, but knew she wasn't thinking clearly. No one was going to identify themselves and she found the voice's willingness to elaborate about the details disconcerting.

"When you've acquired the key, call this number back," he—she assumed it was a male—finished before ending the connection, ignoring her last question.

Audible frustration and fear clawed at her throat. This was coming from Jerrod, cars and converters being targeted, but it was risky. Abnormally risky with a far greater margin of error. Bordering on unhinged—which he never was.

Setting all the problems aside, she was again faced with two choices. Both options left her with the potential for getting arrested thus putting an end to her association with all those involved. And she could see no way out of either.

Summer waited until Katelyn and Ayana eventually cleared out and her chairs were prepared and ready for the morning. Then she moved her car.

A detached sort of autopilot kicked in and had her going through the motions with little emotional interference, steady in the midst of drowning in yet another tempest sea. She'd done nothing to discredit Katelyn's questions as to why she was acting so weird—again—only able to keep the end goal in mind. Sidestepping would only last so long before, this too, became a bigger point of contention. But now that the ball was rolling, Summer couldn't worry about her sister too, detachment making multitasking an impossible feat.

And she needed to call Reyes. Like an hour ago but she and Jerrod were the only ones counting the minutes here. Instead of dutifully calling Liam, Summer went back inside, took five deep breaths, then pulled up Five Star Towing's number. No one answered on the first try, enough of a deterrent to make her put the phone back down. Another few breaths in and out helped steady her hand to pick it back up.

Someone eventually answered after the third try. "I need to report a vehicle that's violating my business parking," she began without preamble, like if she said the words fast enough, no one would detect the deception. After reciting her tag number, the gruff response informed her that they would be out there whenever they would be out there.

With the screen now blank, the first part in place, Summer went and stood at the front door, looking out through the glass at her own car, which had every right to be there.

Not the point, she forced herself to remember. The problem was, she kept losing sight of what the right points were. Continuing to tell herself it didn't matter, she acknowledged that she was also avoiding the next step, because it was becoming steadily apparent that the last thing she wanted to talk to Liam about was anything related to Jerrod.

How had it have come to this, where the man who'd used her, monitored her, made her life not her own, was now the person she wanted to know outside of all that, removed from all that? Shaking her head as though it could scatter the cobbled thoughts residing there, she drew out her phone. She could do hard things. She'd been doing them all along and this was no different. It couldn't be.

Reyes answered rather tersely, "Summer."

"Hey, I need a minute," she responded anxiously, trying to drown out the running narrative in her mind.

"A quick one."

"Well, I hope you've got more than that to spare because I need you. I need your help," she amended quickly, resulting in the briefest, yet tense, pause.

"I thought you were at the clinic."

"Still am. I'm finished with clients and Katelyn's orientation, but one of Jerrod's people just called and I've been pulled into another job."

"Fuck," he muttered.

"I thought you needed me to keep being involved?"

"I do. We do," he added before another terse interval. "But, fuck."

"Yeah, I feel you, trust me."

Even if she wanted to press and find out what exactly was bothering him about this, there simply was no time. Then, on impulse, she considered an alternative. "Will you come with me? This may come as a shock, but I don't know how to steal actual things."

With a mix of irritation and amusement, he asked, "They want *you* to take the target this time? Why?"

"I don't know but it's slightly more complicated—and not at all funny—what they are asking me to do. I just got off the phone with this archaic towing company and am waiting, as we speak, for them to come tow my own car out of my own designated parking spot."

"Okay…" He drew out the syllable, clearly missing the picture.

"Once they take it, I'm to go to the tow yard and get it back," she explained impatiently. "And while I'm there, help myself to their gate key."

"Gate key? As in an actual, metal key?"

"That's my impression. That's why I said they were archaic, apparently, the lot is armed with the good old padlock kind, which is why I was told to use this specific company. I'm guessing Jerrod, or somebody, did a reconnaissance trip before setting all this up otherwise

174

how would they know about what kind of lock they use?"

"Without a doubt he checked. No matter how pissed he is at you for blowing him off the other night, he wouldn't waste time if there wasn't potential for a lucrative result. And this stays consistent with the story he gave you about the converters. But still...this doesn't fit his usual style."

"You're right, no matter how mad he is, if this wouldn't garner profit, he wouldn't waste his time just to mess with me. But yeah, there's something off about it, whatever the reason he wants me to commit the theft," she theorized, though it felt too intangible an idea saying it out loud and have it make sense to someone who didn't know him like she did. Anyone except Liam.

"I don't wonder."

"Why's that?"

"Think about it. A beautiful female, alone, probably upset—or at least inconvenienced—going in to get her impounded vehicle would draw far less suspicion and possibly elicit greater distraction. Anyone can canvass the area, mark the weak spots. This plan puts someone directly inside, someone who won't raise concern."

She did not want to feel all glowy for being called beautiful, especially over the reason why he was saying it, but even misplaced...the words felt wonderful. "Thanks, I think. Still, not sure why they don't just sneak in and take care of it or break down the lock, or—" Sucking in a breath, Summer stopped mid-sentence.

She could hear Liam in her ear repeatedly calling her name when she didn't finish the ramble but his voice didn't break through the clutch of dread that took over as she watched the truck pull to a stop behind her crossover.

It wasn't the fast arrival of the tow truck that threw

her off. No, it was the fact that the person driving the truck looked vaguely, yet unnervingly, familiar.

Chapter Seventeen

"You really don't know who he is or how you know him?"

"No. Sorry, I don't," she repeated for what felt like the hundredth time.

She was riding shotgun for Liam as he took an intentionally indirect route to Five Star's lot. While he bought them some time, she wracked her mind about how or where she might know the truck driver.

In true Reyes' fashion, he wasn't satisfied with her "I don't know" responses. The problem was, she really couldn't place the driver, even if her instincts insisted they had crossed paths before. "I'm very annoyed at myself right now, without your annoyance adding to it. As soon as I figure it out, you'll be the first one I tell. Besides, what good would it do to hide how I know someone?"

His eyes arced in her direction, confirming with an expression what she already figured he was thinking.

Sighing, she squared her shoulders, "Just because something about him makes my stomach flip like he's bad karma, doesn't mean I can wrongly accuse him of anything. I honestly don't remember him. It's an impression of having seen his face before or of it reminding me of someone else. I can't jump to a conclusion that it's related to Jerrod or this entire nightmare based off a vibe."

Without an immediate response, she figured he was chewing over the logic of what she'd said, debating its level of transparency. Discomfort settled along her spine and had her shifting in the seat.

After what she'd revealed about the money, how was that not enough to garner his trust or earn his acceptance? But she still dodged aspects of the truth, so how could she value his belief in her? Trust and truth were twisty things, ready to bend another to their righteous version given the opportunity. That didn't stop her desire for his faith in her.

As far as the mystery truck driver was concerned and considering the visceral reaction she'd experienced on seeing him, it burned not to be able to remember better. Her memory didn't usually fail if it was something important, but the more she forced herself to try to identify him, the more blurry the driver's face became. Saddled with remorse, disillusioned by lack of clarity, their arrival at the tow yard came quicker than was expected.

Nervously, Summer fiddled with the seatbelt before blurting out something she instantly regretted, "Are you married?"

This time he turned fully instead of just giving her a side eye. "Are you kidding?"

"Sorry, girlfriend…whatever," she mumbled, mortified at her stupid mouth.

A glint of temper lanced across his face. "No. I'm single. Not sure what about any of this would make you think I'm committed to somebody else."

"It's just…yeah. I don't know."

"Don't project your lack of trust in men onto all others who cross your path."

"I don't have a specific lack of trust in men. Necessarily."

"Call it what you want," he said. "Anyone who's been through what you've been though would naturally build defenses, would question things. I get it. I still don't belong in that category."

"There's a clear reason why I don't know anything about you, a reason why the moment you disappear out my door, I'm not supposed to know anything else that happens. The night at the bar was a fluke, wasn't it? You weren't supposed to see me outside of the job."

His jaw tightened again, accompanied by a brief nod of agreement, "That line I'm not supposed to cross keeps growing thinner."

She shook her head, acknowledging the inevitable. "But not thin enough. Look, you have nothing to prove to me, Liam. As long as we're all trying to do the best we can to end this, that's all there is to give."

She wanted to harness it, take control, and remind her heart that it didn't want fresh pain. But after everything that had whittled it down to a throbbing, aching mess, there were still stubborn shards of hope that simply would not give up on the potential of what might be. The icy blocks of protection were slipping and melting despite the reason she'd just supplied. Disappearing at rapid speed to leave her heart bare and vulnerable yet again.

"Hey, if you can fool your worthless ex-husband into thinking that you would actually grace him with your presence again, I think you can handle the tow guy. You've got this."

Summer looked up to see a smile tugging at his beautiful lips. Funny how she used to think them too harsh to be anything but cruel. Yet, she knew firsthand how soft and tempting they could feel. Now that hidden tenderness graced the curves of his mouth, in an attempt she knew was purposeful for lightening her spirit, for making her feel like there *could* be an end to the madness.

"Are you saying you think I'm too good for Jerrod?"

"Definitely. *Way* too good."

They got out and started walking and while she didn't think herself capable of being lighthearted at the moment, she shot him a grin over her shoulder, truly grateful that he was with her and she didn't have to do this alone.

Then, another disturbing thought occurred to her. "What if Jerrod's still got eyes on this place? It would be something he'd do, covering all bases, making sure I don't screw up even if he's still supremely pissed. If they see you with me…that may not go well."

"I have no illusions that he doesn't have surveillance posted up around here and when he questions you, which we know he will, you should use the same story we created for your mom and sister. I'm a new client who happened to be your last client of the day. And when you discovered your car had been towed by mistake, I so graciously offered you a ride over here."

Feasibility-wise, it could work but she didn't want to assume Jerrod would drop his suspicions and obsessions so easily. "Do you really think that will satisfy him? I was instructed to wait until *all* patients were gone, not call it in before the clinic was good and empty. Because on a hit, every detail counts, complete compliance is crucial."

"Tell him I surprised you, came back after hours for

something I'd left next to a chair. As for the task at hand, how we play it to the truck driver or whomever else we run into, take your cues from me."

And here she'd just been feeling grateful for his help. This didn't feel like helping so much as dictating— again. Then, she considered her inexperience and was able to keep matching his pace across the lot with a certain amount of gratitude.

With moderate patience, she succeeded in keeping her mouth shut as they walked to the entrance, loosely together but nothing to indicate great familiarity. Scanning the grounds, she took in the semi-derelict building adjacent to a tall, gated area, with approximately a third full of vehicles lined up along the patches of crumbling asphalt. A scrap of shade came from an ancient oak, one whose trunk had grown wide enough to put pressure against a portion of the chain links. Overall, a place she would rather avoid.

So, it surprised her to see a portion of the impounded cars looked expensive, which was silly. Having a pricey ride didn't mean having an exemption in tow zones. As she completed her own assessment of the place, Summer noticed the elusive scanning Liam was doing as well, all while exuding an air of careless annoyance.

When they got to the door, he didn't try to open it for her. Curiosity further piqued at his angle, she tugged on the handle and propped it open so he could file in after her. Once they were inside, he moved up behind her, placed his fingers against the small of her back and guided her to the counter. The move noted possession; she tried her best to block the heat his touch brought to her system, but it spread anyway, melting into her bones.

Alone in the reception area, he took the opportunity

to lean in. "Remember, follow my lead."

Taking a purposeful step to the side, his distance took the heightened air with him. She started to voice questions about the plan but a muffled noise from somewhere in the recesses told her to keep silent. A few beats later, a hard-faced woman emerged, letting an interior door snap shut behind her as she made her way over to where an old monitor was affixed behind the tall wall of Formica. Eyeing down the new arrivals, her features didn't soften.

"Help you?" She addressed them gruffly, noticeably staring at the way Liam kept a hand nestled at Summer's back.

"Sure can," he replied easily, in direct contrast to her abrasiveness, while guiding Summer forward the remaining distance to the counter.

An underlying southern accent came out to color his voice. She struggled not to turn and catch a glimpse of his expression. A chameleon, she realized. He could become what he needed to be, whatever the job required. Regardless of what his face must have looked like, Summer remained forward facing and watched the woman regard him with an adapted level of speculation.

"My girl here went and got her car towed," he drawled. "Can't believe we have to deal with this shit right now but hey." His tone was a verbal eye roll and she saw the woman return it with a literal eye roll of her own.

"Happens to the best of us," she finally conceded, sending him what looked to Summer to be a hard-won attempt at a smile.

Damn, the man could make nearly anyone crack, even this crusty, harsh faced worker. And here she'd thought she would need to be the one who turned it on, assuming the person they would deal with was heterosexual male. The only thing she needed to portray now was the supporting role of a flighty girlfriend inconveniencing her annoyed boyfriend.

While Liam chatted with their gatekeeper, Summer focused on the wall behind the woman, searching for a rack of keys. The lobby was sparse, boasting only two scratched metal chairs set at a right angle to the workstation. Clearly, they didn't want anyone to feel encouraged enough to hang out longer than absolutely necessary.

The height of the counter made it impossible for her to entirely see what was behind it and when she did attempt to lean forward a bit to try and see over the side, Reyes sent her a swift but unmistakable warning glance. Anxiety had her toes twitching to walk around and track down the target. How was she supposed to nab something she couldn't find?

When he shot out one arm, blocking her from further snooping, she whined, "Can we just get the car already? You know we have dinner plans tonight and I have to have time to get ready."

Humor intended only for her lit up his eyes as he turned his head. "Yeah, honey, sorry. We're taking care of paying up right now."

The annoyed boyfriend was now doting, indulging the fact that his girlfriend wanted to leave. Reyes withdrew his wallet, produced a card along with an under the breath comment sounding suspiciously like why she had to go and park the car where she shouldn't have in the first place and then they wouldn't be late for dinner, causing the woman to chuckle. Reyes paid the dues before subsequently being escorted out a side exit, presumably leading to the lot, leaving her alone in the lobby.

As much as she wanted to launch over the counter and start digging into whatever waited on the other side, during her visual sweep of the lobby, she'd seen the lone security camera affixed in the far corner, aimed directly at the space she sought to rummage through.

Stealing a fast glance out the dingy side window, Summer saw the internal access from the building to the car lot was open, with Liam and the woman standing just inside the chain link fence, still chatting. But the conversation was taking on a more one-sided quality. He was trying to buy her time, and she just prayed it would be long enough before the woman ended the exchange.

It was hard not to look back at the camera, but she succeeded in keeping her head down as she bit the bullet and pushed forward through the hinged half door separating the lobby space. She waited a few precious seconds to make sure someone wouldn't come barreling in and call her out for being back there, but no one must have been actively monitoring the camera because after pausing for those moments of reassurance, she was still alone.

The counter lacked any clear organization but wasn't overly cluttered. The computer where payments were rung up was a dinosaur desktop model with an ancient tower turned on its side so that the thick screen could sit on top of it. Two filing cabinets stood against the far wall, right beneath the camera. But none of these details really mattered because she still did not see the gate key.

Knowing the window of opportunity was rapidly

shrinking, Summer kept her face turned down and marched over to what she assumed was a back office or storage area. She was starting to feel desperate now, so drastic measures were needed. Just as she was about to raise her fist to knock, the door abruptly swung open, annihilating the assumption that she wasn't being watched.

"What're you doing back here?"

Chapter Eighteen

The man in front of her was broad, burly and eyed her with suspicion from beneath dark, bushy eyebrows laced with wiry, gray strands. For whatever reason, Summer was instantly grateful that it was not the same trucker who'd caused her such upset back at Longtime Sun. That didn't mean she was in the clear though.

She said the first thing that came to mind, punctuating the request with a feminine purse of her lips. "I need to use the bathroom, please."

He paused, giving her an unimpressed once over, then jerked his head to the side, indicating the direction from which he'd just appeared. "Back out there if you really have to."

She had no intentions of using the facilities in a place that almost guaranteed having cleanliness standards beneath her comfort level but amped up her smile and moved forward so he would step aside and let her through. What she would do once she got back there, Summer had no clue, but aimlessly wandering the front lobby wasn't getting her anywhere.

Just as she was easing by his bulk that was still semi-blocking the doorway, he stopped her by lifting one of his thick arms. Invisible ants of worry scurried down her limbs. She wouldn't be able to search in the back areas after all. Somehow, he knew she was a fraud…

"You'll need these."

And just like that, the ants receded as he held out a heavy metal key ring that held several keys. Trying not to grin like an idiot, Summer latched onto the key he'd used to hand the ring over with, presumably because it was the bathroom key. Remembering to school her face, she leveled her mouth while looking up and found his attention wasn't even on her, having already dismissed her along with the keys.

Grabbing onto the newfound luck, she fast walked the short distance down the narrow hall that led to the outside. Resisting the urge to look out toward the lot and locate Liam again, Summer quickly unlocked the door to the gas station style free standing restroom located behind the main building. Once inside—and yes, her suspicions of sub-par cleaning were indeed confirmed—she stood in the middle of the hot, cramped space, rapidly turning each key over in her palm. They weren't labeled in any sort of fashion.

Feeling the biting pressure, the nerves that wanted to take control, she refused to let them engulf her. Slowing down, starting again, Summer inspected each key thoroughly, looking at both sides and assessing the shape. When she'd narrowed it down to two possibilities for the gate based on size, she was assailed by the sound of the heavy metal door slamming, followed by footfalls crunching over disintegrating concrete.

She'd run out of time.

Closing her eyes and clutching at her courage, Summer hastily undid one of the two options from the ring and zipped the unidentified key into the pouch in her satchel.

****

Liam insisted they get some dinner before she

delivered the key.

To not immediately give Jerrod what he had propositioned her for was a risky move, but Reyes made it hard to say no. They soon were driving outside Savannah toward the beaches of Tybee Island. The change of scene brought about a renewed sense of peace, something Summer hadn't felt since the last time she and Liam been alone together.

With the pace notched back, and their anonymity relatively safe, they settled into patio chairs situated on the sandy deck of a beach café. When Liam ordered a beer, she followed suit with his apparent desire to further unwind for the interim.

"Sit back and enjoy for a while." He sent her a reaffirming smile. "Take the opportunity; we both know the next phase won't be easy for you."

She found it easy to match his affect and leaned back against the low-slung chair. They hadn't spoken again about her decision not to return to Jerrod the other night. She suspected that if he did voice his opinion on the matter, it would either pose direct conflict with orders or very effectively push her away. Her perception of his conflict over her and their situation was becoming a daily evolution.

"I'm still impressed that you could sweet talk that bitter woman. Were you thinking she had the key?" Summer asked once their drinks had been delivered, and their server was out of earshot.

Taking a healthy swig, Liam assumed a similarly lax position across from her. "It's less to do with me and more on being able to read people."

When she arched a brow, he elaborated, "If you can figure out what people are after, what irritates them, or what they covertly want, it is so much easier to play on those things. Most people are dissatisfied with something or someone, so that's usually the most tender and effective spot to nudge."

The notion of how well he could read her, of his ability to target *her* tender spots, prodded at her ease with the moment. Shifting against the rising tightness in her chest, she took a small sip. "How could you have figured out what her wants and needs were in the whole five minutes we spent in there talking to her?"

Scrubbing a palm along the facial scruff he'd let grow longer over the last few days, he shrugged up a shoulder in a way that one would take as indifference. In fact, it spoke to a healthy confidence she'd come to grudgingly admire. Because he was neither indifferent nor ostentatious, but some combination comprised of all the things that were uniquely Liam.

"She's annoyed by stupidity, which is ironic considering the clientele she must deal with on a regular basis," he said. "Then she saw you, pretty and young, being *led in* by me. As soon as I insinuated, you'd done something dumb, she jumped on it. All I had to do was play the hand of irritated boyfriend, cleaning up his ditzy girlfriend's fuck up and she was more open to talking."

"That's kind of offensive but, okay. What about her secret wants and desires?" Summer asked curiously, only half joking.

He was quiet for a moment, watching her intently, "It would have taken me a bit longer to uncover those, and time was not on our side."

"Fair enough. I guess it doesn't matter anyway, though, since I got the key."

"That you did. At least, *a* key. Now all we can do is

hope your hunch was correct and Metzinger gets what he's after, so you don't face any fallout. Or maybe getting caught at the gate would be exactly what we need to nail him and end this."

"You mean if the key is the wrong one?"

"Yes," he said, almost apologetically, as though reminding her of potential failure was difficult.

Summer didn't need reminders or apologies. She was well versed in many variations of negative self-talk. Although, if one were wise, one would call that being a realist. Before those thoughts could fully manifest and damper their coveted change of pace, he reached over and brushed a thumb across her knuckles in a simple touch that packed a punch. It was probably purposeful, but that touch effectively ended the vein of the conversation as he steered toward personal topics.

With minimal encouragement, Summer shared how she had fallen in love with the art of acupuncture while considering a traditional nursing program and her instant connection with healing through traditional Chinese methods.

In response to her openness, he surprised her further by talking about his family beyond what she knew already of his father. He had a grandfather who was a first-generation Spaniard who moved to the United States from Spain as a child. His mother, also attempting to restart her life after losing a spouse, was currently based out of Charlotte, staying close by his brother and sister-in-law to help with their growing family.

It frightened her a bit, the way he could *almost* make her forget that her life was being held hostage, that she was operating in a constant state of damage control. He could keep her grounded in the present and provide a reprieve by allowing her to simply be herself outside of their regular context. Had she not been a former criminal and he not be assigned to her case, perhaps their connection could have taken them somewhere beyond their immediate situation.

But even as that notion flowed through her mind, Summer knew she was deluding herself. Liam Reyes was a boldly confident yet serious man with many layers while she kept too many of her own buried inside, battered and bruised.

It was best *not* to forget.

In this post-divorce context, she didn't know how to truly open up to anyone. Or how to let someone in without exposing her torment and the one thing she could never forgive herself for. Keira's death shouldn't be anyone else's burden to shoulder. There was no reason to share those layers. So that meant there was absolutely nothing transparent between her and Liam, even if what she wanted was to let him help her forget all the things that impeded on her gaining a better future.

The text inevitably chimed, interrupting her relative contentment. Reality crashed down with the one-line message.

"It's him," she answered when Reyes' expression became instantly neutral with barely perceivable threads of expectation. Funny, that she could pick and pluck them out easier now.

What she didn't expect to find was something akin to frustration, highlighted through the minute flexing of his jawline. "You knew you would be summoned at some point. His decision that it's time to pay up has arrived."

"Yeah," she sighed, laden with regret. "It was just

nice to let go for a while. Like usual, you did a good job making that happen."

Regret then stiffened into something sharper, something vicious in her gut, making her want to curl in on herself. So quickly, she had chosen to disregard the roles they played, the layers they hid. In defiance to the desire to bend for him, Summer arched her back, sat up ramrod straight. "You seem to always figure out how to get something out of me."

The dig felt false, forced, but when his chin clinched further, she saw that her mark had stung, at least to a degree. "Nothing you weren't willing to give," he finally said, the brittleness of his tone like grated rock against steel.

Good, fine. If it took his ire, whatever was needed to always, always remember those stupid, pointless lies her loneliness tried to feed her. Vying for feeling, oversight for the sake of connection. Affection. Each of those falsehoods thrummed in her head, like a gavel smack with a guilty sentence. Yet she struggled to find true conviction in the need for protection. Was that really all it was? All they were?

When she saw him watching her, evidence clear of such a brutal, internal war, she feigned a small smile, "Don't worry, I'm not desperate enough to forget reality. I'll get Jerrod his key, and then maybe we can get him."

At least her regrets at this moment were not about her ex-husband.

The real possibility of closure was enough to bolster her fortitude during their drive back to the city. He asked no more questions, nor did he allow the intimacy of their break at the restaurant to creep back in. All agent again, while she battened up her guard once more.

After Reyes parked streetside in vicinity of the instructed location, Summer remained focused on that one, particularly important point. They could end this. End all the lies, all the shame that relived itself on an endless loop. End all the reasons to ever see any of these people again...

The thought of Liam being gone for good caused an ache in parts of her that would need to be examined, extracted. The longing she fought to contain, for something that could never be anything, would eventually have to be torn apart and dissected. But not now. Not when her freedom felt much, much closer.

Although he had put the car in park, he'd yet to kill the ignition. Gazing forward out the windshield, Reyes refrained from making eye contact. "You've got the address, right? You know how to get there?"

"Yeah," she said quietly. "It's only a couple of blocks from here." He knew that already, just like she knew he wouldn't be going with her. "Where will you be while I do this?"

"There's business I need to attend to."

"FBI business?"

"Business."

"Liam..."

"Does it matter, Summer? You have to do this part yourself so there's no further connection made between you and me. Going together was a gamble because you know Metzinger—or someone—saw me at the lot. We can't give him any more by letting him see me here too. He'll know too much, suspect too much."

"I know we have to separate," she answered softly, meaning running deeper. "You and me...this. It's too—"

Unable to finish, when Reyes wouldn't turn around, she jammed a hand into her bag, feeling the weight of the key and all it represented as she gripped it between her fingers. Even if he wanted to be evasive over where he was going, she couldn't shake the beams of hope hooking inside her chest. Their newfound alliance couldn't matter right now because the release that could come with the success of the delivery was everything.

Ready to go shove the key down whatever hole Jerrod wanted, the metal burning freedom through her fingers, she pushed open the door and left behind Reyes without a goodbye.

Keying the address given by the AI generated voice into her app, Summer confirmed the remaining walking distance wasn't that far from where Reyes had dropped her. And something else caught her attention. There was a populated store listing for the address of suites—and EarthScapes was identified as one of the businesses in the row.

She wasn't sure why it bothered her that Jerrod had relocated or opened a new business front, but it played on the pride she still held in her previous investment on the legitimate side of the company. Was he playing with funds? Or had someone come digging a little too close and he needed to reinforce the guise of a credible operation? Considering the company name was still intact and the existence of the first location was currently unknown, that intention seemed off. Attempting to discern the reasons behind the move held little point, however, and she needed to get going.

With swift strides, Summer crossed the remaining blocks before slowing her approach as the building came into view. Walking up with caution, she noted the darkened glass of closed-up suites, and it stirred a warning deep in her senses.

She was alone, with stolen property, technically trespassing.

Stealing a few glances in either direction, she confirmed that the only tenant with lights on for early evening hours was in the end suite, unlike the others adjacent to the one she was told to be at. Fewer witnesses, less accountability.

Inching closer to the EarthScapes door, the rush of apprehension grew more urgent—both from the fact the building was ultimately deserted and from the realization that a security camera was angled directly at her face above the entrance. Not only was she breaking a few more laws, she was being documented while doing so. Beyond the recording, another sort of game was unfolding, one that had her feeling like a mouse being toyed with by a diabolical cat. Jerrod wanted to flex his claws, and she wanted to flee the scene.

Instead, she shot as much of a defiant look as she could project directly into the camera. Who knew if he was currently watching, but it felt vital to put up some protest to the role of mouse. Fishing the key out, Summer dangled it in front of the lens, then slipped it through the classic mail slot before striding away, smart enough to know when to fear the cat.

With the key gone and her muted reflection out of recording range, Summer breathed a bit easier. But now, finally alone, a fresh wave of awareness swept in by degrees, swelling up feelings that overwhelmed all she had set out to do. Completion of the task brought the threat of idle time, leaving nothing but her shadowy faults as companions.

Another inhalation, followed by a deep, bruising exhalation. Why did it always come down to shadows, to ghosts? Phantoms of a past that, no matter how hard she tried, could never be rewritten?

She wasn't a power-driven person, she wasn't overly competitive, yet she'd battled over the last year and a half like she was both of those things. She had fought for emancipation and independence, most of all away from her former self.

Was it only to prove that she could survive without anyone's help? On one level, she allowed her family's support, but only on one level. She didn't want to need anyone again but that's exactly what she feared was happening.

Somehow, over the past weeks, she'd shed slices of that fanatical self-reliance. Obsessive independence and the need to prove her worth didn't feel quite so critical when she was with Liam. And it scared her. She had begun to need him and that felt unacceptable in the light of revelation. Liam's ruthlessly controlled passion was a well of discovery that she could barely restrain the need to tap. To unleash.

She had begun to need even more than that. His mixed messages disguised unwavering reliability, even when she knew he was internally at war, just like her. Even when she knew it was partially from her own doing, part of her didn't care, because it meant that maybe she could reach out and brush some of that fire he concealed with some of her own. Brandishing a twin flame so bright, it could consume them both even as it melded them together. She'd nearly told him it was too much, the two of them were too much, but what it really felt was like she couldn't get enough.

She needed his wit, his cockiness and the way he always held himself to such high standards.

She needed Liam.

But she had no idea if he needed her and that was terrifying.

To *want* to let him in, after everything she'd told herself was just too insurmountable, it was excruciating not to know how he thought of her in return. Ruthlessly, she reminded herself that his feelings for her, if they did exist, were based on limited understanding.

A dash of harsh reality blasted through her senses as she nearly walked beyond the crosswalk, too lost to register the darkness cascading down. A swift honk came as a wake up. Wake up, damn it.

It was time to get a fucking grip, because if she didn't, thoughts of all the things that could never be would finally, finally consume her. And she wasn't quite ready to succumb to the losses.

Chapter Nineteen

A full week passed after the key drop with no sign of a hit on the tow yard.

Frustration was an understatement which wouldn't ease because Summer detected the same impatience from Liam the few times they'd spoken over the phone.

She managed appointments during the day then returned home, shackled with an unrelenting hope he would be there, waiting for her. Yet the townhouse sat empty, save her loneliness. Plagued by memories of where he'd touched her with such desire, taken her with such want, failed to lose their intensity.

Summer refused to ask why he hadn't returned or if he even planned to.

Katelyn, having been out for the duration of the week after the impact of her latest radiation treatment, helped direct some attention by assisting with the demand at the front desk in between Ayana's shifts.

Keeping herself engaged with work was one of the best ways to banish the stagnation, the destructive internal dialogue. By the time the next weekend rolled into the following Monday, Summer felt fatigued in a way she hadn't experienced since the early months during Longtime Sun's inception. It was a choice to ignore that she was neglecting her physical body's demands in an effort to counterbalance the condition of her mental health.

Yet, in the first moments of calm, Summer sat at the front desk in the early hours, sipping coffee, trying to be still. When that didn't suffice, she scrolled through upcoming appointments on the tablet. Idle swiping turned into double checking a file for a patient whom she hadn't treated in a while along with the approval of a handful of last-minute bookings for the following morning. This was good, this was productive.

No clients were officially due in for another hour, but Ayana had volunteered to arrive earlier than usual in order to make up time for having left early on one of her shifts last week. So, while she didn't need to be here quite so soon, her head decided differently. When there were no more tasks to complete, no more excuses to make, she eventually let the tablet settle onto her lap, coffee mug placed within reach.

Her mind wandered, against her best intentions, and shockingly, her body settled enough that what felt like only seconds later, she was startled by Ayana, noisily making her way through the front and being uncharacteristically loud about it. Oblivious to her boss dozing at the desk, she unloaded a water canteen and earbuds from a heavily filled carryall, dropping them down sharply onto the space beside Summer's coffee.

The clatter of items on the wood expelled any lingering grogginess and she narrowed her eyes, assessing Ayana's movements as the girl clumsily rummaged through her purse. "Hey, Ayana. You okay?"

She jerked back like Summer had swung on her. "What? Hey, sorry," she answered absently before resuming her search.

"No problem. Just want to make sure you're good. You know, you didn't have to come in early if you weren't up for it, you could have just flexed your hours another day this week," Summer spoke calmly, reasonably, not pointing out that *she* had ended up coming in early and had already completed the opening set up.

Misplaced irritation reared up. Why would she even be here now if she was just going to be flustered, distracted by whatever was dragging her assistant through her bag.

"It's not that," Ayana's voice sounded muffled while she kept her head down during the hunt. Then, as if finally realizing that Summer was expressing concern masked annoyance, she stopped pawing through the purse and straightened enough to make eye contact. "How's Katelyn doing?"

Summer paused, arching a brow at the change of direction. But she bit down the comment and instead rose and walked over to the beverage stand to top off her coffee. "She's finally getting some energy back and wants to try to be back at work by the end of the week."

Ayana looked relieved. "That's great. I mean, for her and for us. It's just…we've really been busy."

Busyness had never really seemed to faze her before. Thoughtfully, Summer leaned back, mug in hand, studying her face. "Her involvement with social media seems to be paying off. That's what she's been intermittently working on from home."

Ayana hummed some kind of approval or agreement before announcing that she was heading to the back to prep the linens.

The hand she raised was poised to stop her, to tell her everything was already done. But, following her suspicions, Summer refrained. Instead, she waited until she walked away before she did something that violated her fundamental beliefs regarding employees. However, if whatever was making Ayana act suspicious and twitchy was an illegal substance, that was grounds for immediate firing.

Besides, she only intended to look, not touch.

Standing on tiptoe so she could get a full shot of the opened purse without using her hands, Summer scanned in between the hairbrush, cosmetics bag and other random items. Nothing glaring popped out, no plastic bags or paraphernalia. Nothing controversial. Breathing out, she eased away, unsure of what to do now. Was she let down by the lack of incriminating evidence? The lack of, well, something to tackle? Perhaps she really should take a break if she was going to stoop so low as to try and nail her front desk girl for possession.

Just as she was about to back away and chalk up the erratic behavior to sleep deprivation, something tucked into an interior pocket caught her eye. A business card, one that had been slid into the sleeve nearly all the way in and if it had been pushed completely down, she would never have seen it. But the corners were just visible enough to expose a familiar symbol of a half palm leaf eclipsing a sun emblazoned on one end.

A symbol that she had come to loathe.

****

"So, what are we going to do about it?" She felt the words explode out of her lungs as she paced her living room while Liam sat watching her, armed with an annoying cloak of calm.

Night had pushed in and the only light she bothered to set was the fireplace, adding darkness to her mood. Since finding the card for EarthScapes in Ayana's purse, she felt the steady unraveling of her composure, surely like she was losing her mind. And nothing about that came close to matching his level of calm. As angered as she was, it was also attached to a multitude of underlying threads. Like bafflement and violation. In that one, blinding blast of Jerrod's logo being present in *her* space, it felt as if everything she'd fought to establish, all semblance of a normal, detached life was about to be ripped apart by one man, one organization. If that made her irrational, bordering on explosive, she didn't really care. That's the way those feelings festered and as that anger and fear simmered to a boiling point, her counterpart in this whole mess remained unflappably serene. At least he'd come when she'd sought him out.

"We will do nothing at the moment," Reyes lifted a hand just as she was about to reiterate—quite vehemently—her justifications. "But analyze the facts," he added with enough force to make her think he wasn't all that unaffected.

"Analyze the facts," she repeated incredulously, unable to stop the compulsive torrent of emotions. It wasn't okay. Nothing about this felt okay.

Snapping her head up, she glared into the pretense he held up against her swirling daggers. "Okay. Yes. Let's analyze. How about this? Somehow my conniving psychopath of an ex has managed to groom my employee. He's managed, yet again, to sink his insidious hooks into someone who has no idea how much destruction it will cause."

"We don't have any proof that she's done anything, only that she was carrying the card."

"Well, how much more fucking proof do we need? A neon fucking sign that says I agreed to do his dirty work? Because, excuse me, but why the hell else would she even have an association with a yard company? I know this girl lives in an apartment and doesn't appear to have any inclination toward gardening, pruning, whatever. Anything that would remotely constitute the need to hire a landscaping company."

"Maybe it isn't for her. Maybe someone she knows is in the market for some lawn care and she was simply scoping out options, but I take it that nugget of reasoning is inconsequential right now."

Damn right. A swift nod confirmed what he had already deduced because no amount of reasonability could quell the never-ending roll of dread twisting up her stomach. It was entirely plausible that she had the card for someone else. But it didn't *feel* right, her instincts screaming otherwise. And if he was bent on having such a civilized discussion, those instincts would heighten their shrill beating.

"Has there ever been any time you two have discussed Metzinger? Does she have any knowledge about what's gone down between you or any details of the relationship, like a male-bashing session or something?"

"Ha ha and no, nothing like that. I hired Ayana well after we were officially divorced so the only thing she knows is that I have an ex-husband named Jerrod. No company name, no disclosures for bashing. Just a name and a general category. Besides, she's too inexperienced to understand, even if I did have a desire to emasculate anyone."

He had the gall to flash a grin, which, weirdly, helped to settle her distress a bit. "Hmm, okay, maybe not your first go-to person for emasculation but maybe not as inexperienced as she's allowed you to think." Summer knew the incredulousness shown on her face when he expanded further, "Or perhaps she is that clueless and has no idea that the person—company— she's looking into has anything to do with her boss's history. Which takes us right back around to the wait and see part you don't like."

"You're right, I don't. More bad things happen when you wait around for the train to hit you instead of proactively jumping off the tracks."

Another smile shone on his face at the analogy, one that held affection. She felt her unease settle more, no longer pounding quite so insidiously beneath her skin. Breath entered her lungs with more clarity as his warmth reminded her she wouldn't be handling this alone.

"But then why was she acting so weird if there's nothing to hide?"

"That's the question, isn't it? And you're saying that type of behavior is out of character for her?"

"Mostly she can just be a little flighty," Summer sighed. "I mean, she's young, going to school for graphic design, and was looking for part time receptionist type work at the time when I posted the job. We've had no issues other than a few times when I've had to accommodate her class schedule or if she's got a serious assignment with a hard deadline, but again, that's usually a nonissue and can be worked around easily enough."

"Because you're always there to pick up the slack. I'm glad you brought Katelyn on," he murmured, reaching up to lightly trace the dark circles under her eyes with the pads of his thumbs. The unexpected touch shimmered heat through her pores. The resulting shiver was unavoidable, and his eyes flashed hungrily in response.

Unsure of him, of herself, Summer inched a tiny, deliberate step backward. He dropped his hands but the heat in his gaze didn't lessen. "We can't rule out that the odd behavior correlates to the possession of Metzinger's card. Neither can we assume that it does, though."

"That's just basically saying we have no idea why it's there or what she's doing."

"Precisely. And until we know more, we wait."

"You're infuriating sometimes, you know that?"

"Of course. But you'd really be infuriated if you confronted her, laid the whole ugly debacle out on the line and came to find out that she was oblivious to the entire situation."

"Infuriating and smart."

"I feel exactly the same way about you."

She felt the potent pull, being helplessly drawn in to him. She wanted to be held, nearly as much as she wanted answers—with breath-stealing intensity.

"You've been gone."

Statement, not question.

"I'm sorry."

Apology, not honesty.

And it scared her that she *almost* didn't care about his lack of truth. All the revelations from the week before only felt further magnified as he aimed that liquid, molten gaze her way. Her heart rate quickened, lips parted in an attempt to seek his before she could find some semblance of control and press them closed again.

He'd been gone and he hadn't told her why. They'd worked as a team, accomplishing what she'd figured would have been impossible if she had been on her own and then afterward had disappeared. There was no real trust, no true confidence in their collaboration. And all while she'd been on the brink of succumbing to admitting her need for him.

And he could see her shuttering against it, closing down the flow of connection surging between them because his own mouth tightened, bracketing with tension and something else she couldn't completely place.

Before either could speak against the break in energy, an incoming call on his phone jolted them both. For a few heightened seconds, she thought, perhaps, he wouldn't be the one to fracture the unspoken language weaving between them. A terse response of "Reyes" shriveled that thought. He retreated without further comment, the connection severed.

Settling in front of the fireplace with a steaming mug of tea and a book was intentional. Proof that she was fine. She'd been on her own for a while now and would be fine to continue that way. The hollowness of those convictions had already begun to carve deep grooves inside her chest, they threatened to fester there beside the pulsing pieces of her other enduring heartbreak.

Somehow this felt different—it morphed into a new kind of pain, edging into awareness. If only she could encase this, trap it behind walls, it might not be so consuming.

It was late when a simultaneous text and soft knock on the door announced Liam's presence. By then, she was curled up, drifting lightly beneath the fire's muted glow. Startled, she watched him enter, her brain slow to process that he'd used his key. That he had returned.

He knelt beside her, gently tucking the blanket around her with unmistakable tenderness.

"You came back."

"I came back," he affirmed.

The careful avoidance of contact which he'd employed earlier was now gone, replaced by a quiet sort of urgency to be close to her. Reaching up, he smoothed a few strands of hair from her forehead. His hand traced down her arm, igniting shivers. Her breath broke. In response, his grip captured her fingers, before a sharp release, as though he couldn't keep on touching her without consequence.

"Summer, I need to—"

This time, the shattering of intentions came from her phone.

Jerrod.

A flick up to Liam's face reinforced what she'd have to do. It had been too long since she'd heard from him and there was too much at stake. Tearing her eyes away, she answered with an unsteady voice. "Hey."

The line was subtle static for a moment before he spoke with little inflection. "Hey, Summer. Hope I didn't wake you."

His tone was different, his statement misplaced. This wasn't going to end well. She fought to clear her voice of the fog she'd been floating in prior to Liam's arrival. "Not at all. You know me with sleep sometimes."

He rumbled a low sound of agreement in his throat, a lightning-fast switch toward emphasis. Which Jerrod was she dealing with? The detached, calculating man or the one who let temper and desires be in control?

Liam moved close enough to listen in, made a twirling motion with his finger before miming unlocking a door.

"Did you get your delivery all right? I tried to get in

touch after and you know, with the new location and everything…" She let the rambling sentence stall out, paranoid that distracting him would only make things worse.

"Well now, you know I did. Got there just fine." His reply was laced with enough snide that reminded her of the face she'd made into his camera.

Reyes started to move his hands again, gesturing for her to continue. Before she was able to say anything more, Jerrod's voice dropped to a lower timbre. She saw that Reyes couldn't hear as well now and felt ill-equipped to handle this on her own. Funny, when only hours before she'd been feeding herself bullshit, peddling her own independent hype.

"Now that I have you on the phone, *baby,* I want to personally thank you for helping us."

"You don't need to do that," she gritted out, eyes wide on Reyes' face as if she could decipher the code on how to get out of this just by looking at him.

"I think I do because I may be asking for another favor again very soon."

"Does this have to do with Ayana?" Summer blurted, unable to keep the need to know contained. Bracing herself, she shifted uncomfortably at the flicker of astonishment in Reyes' eyes.

"Who?" A wealth of bored awareness coated the singular word.

"You know, the one who works for *me*, Jerrod, not you."

"Ah, the new one you mean." He sighed as though he were the one humoring her. Like he had no idea whom she was referencing but he knew. Just like he knew exactly what he wanted from her. A grand plan, always one step ahead of her and everyone else. She felt like shredding something, preferably the ropes that kept her tethered to this nightmare.

"This favor could involve others," he said. "Or not. Depends on the deal."

"I know. The deal," she answered bitterly. "I also know she's a good kid. Going to school, doing the right thing. She doesn't need to be involved with us."

"Us? Interesting word choice. But you're wrong, Summer, I know exactly what she is—a potential asset, albeit a dispensable one, to what Cameron and I plan to pull off."

"I thought you were going to hit the tow yard."

A beat passed before he responded, "It's important to keep your options open."

Patience straining at the evasion, she said, "Please tell me what my office coordinator has to do with helping you and Cameron. Do you need her for EarthScapes? If so, I can gladly work out her schedule with you. An on the books and documented kind of schedule."

He laughed richly—as though her nervous proposal was funny and her deteriorating composure predictable. "No, not for EarthScapes. Like you said, she's a law-abiding citizen, going to school, keeping her nose clean. Who better to have in our pocket for a little scoping? Allow us to…exercise some privilege while on campus?"

"What are you talking about?"

"You waste my time when you can't keep up. Your little receptionist is going to report on possible hits whenever she travels to and from class. All those shiny, expensive cars bought by overindulgent parents. It'll be a gold mine."

Appalled, Summer exclaimed, "She's just a kid!"
"And?"
"Isn't it wrong to you to use someone so young?"

"Youth has very little to do with financial morality, in my experience. And as it stands, she seems thrilled to bank a little extra cash, presumably unbothered by the nature of this endeavor as much as you might want to shield her otherwise. I have to say, I haven't seen this kind of protective, maternal streak out of you since, well, since…you know. It would be good for you to channel that baby energy elsewhere."

She felt the blood drain from all her extremities, blanching both cheeks, hollowing out all pockets. He had never spoken to her about the miscarriage, not directly anyway. Not even at the hospital. Like it was some *inconvenience* she'd dealt him, a minor blip on his radar.

Her brain funneled words to her mouth; phrases that stumbled over themselves; screams that needed to be heard, yet clashed together, forming a disaster behind her lips.

The moments ticked by, Reyes' gaze steady, waited for…what? A response, an admission that continuously evaded? She breathed, again and again, finally whispering, "Don't you have any guilt, Jerrod? Any remorse, any sadness? Over this…or over what happened?"

"Guilt? Remorse. Sadness." He itemized each emotion as if they were listed on some mundane checklist. "Why would you think that? Nature did what nature does, there's nothing to feel guilty about. If your body couldn't hold it, then it's for the best. Probably wasn't viable anyway…"

The might it took her to hold tight to the sounds that

threatened to rip out of her throat put too much pressure on the calcification in her chest. Clucking the heel of her hand against her sternum, Summer processed that Jerrod was still speaking while Reyes watched her slowly crumble.

It was only after Liam eased the phone away from her ear, spurring her to mumble some semblance of a closing remark—another agreement of assistance—that the disintegration of the walls around her heart sped up their destruction.

Chapter Twenty

The tears from sweeping, raw pain slid steadily down her face. The helpless way Liam sat beside her, their thighs touching, waiting for her to talk was just as raw. Summer had never seen his stature appear so vulnerable. Yet, he remained at her side, witnessing her breakdown with unshielded empathy.

She could be a thousand different versions of herself right now, but the one that needed to show up, the one that mattered was the one who owned her truth.

"I was pregnant at the beginning of last year. Right before I filed for divorce." His leg pressed closer, but comfort was suddenly sticky. She pushed through the heaviness, having come too far to back out now. "At sixteen weeks, I found out it was a girl. I named her Keira."

She took a second to look into his eyes. "I was so thrilled. I would have been happy either way, but a girl just sent me over. You know the quote on the clinic wall? *May the Longtime Sun shine upon you*?"

His nod encouraged her to continue. "I would sing that to her sometimes, when she was safe in my belly. The clinic is dedicated to her. The name…everything."

With his warmth still flush against her, he reached for her hand, drew soft circles with his thumb across the webs of skin between her fingers, the only indication she was crying again. Only now did she feel their sting as her heart bled silent, traumatic tears. She didn't know how to accept his sympathy. Or worse, his pity.

"The day of the gender ultrasound was the day Jerrod said he needed me again. To drive. I'd stupidly thought he would care if we were having a boy or a girl, but he didn't show. He reasonably pointed out that he was working to provide for our family. Or, I guess more accurately, he needed to pick up the slack that I would be leaving behind because I'd told him I wanted out of the field now that I was pregnant." She let out a derisive laugh. "Such an inconvenience I'd caused, like I'd impregnated myself."

The slow circles stopped; his fingers tightened around hers. Maybe restraint was better for them both. "I tried to focus on building his client list by garnering reviews. I reworked the office space, revamped advertising but that's not the way Jerrod operates. He…gets off on the rush of stealing, of manipulating, and would never have let it go no matter how well I ran EarthScapes. I can only say that now, because in the midst of it all, I was still ignorant."

"It's always easier to see once you're removed from it," Liam responded in a low tone, like he was trying to reign himself in.

"Yeah, hindsight and all that," she said. "Hindsight that my marriage was broken way earlier than I knew, hindsight that I was being manipulated just like everyone else he was interacting with."

"So you drove anyway? After you told him no?"

"I drove anyway," she confirmed, bile rising in her throat. "I left the fucking doctor's office to meet Cameron, instead of celebrating with my husband."

"Cameron." A lifetime of meaning applied to that

name now and she could all but see him connecting the mental dots, drawing the damning lines.

"Cameron," she repeated, "was in need of a driver. It was a lucrative hit, a big deal. Instead of nurturing my body like I was supposed to, what I knew was the right thing, I did what Jerrod told me and drove to pick up Cameron from a job."

Even though she had relived these moments over and over, the anguish was still just as crippling as if it were happening in real time. When Summer registered that Liam tightened his grip on her hand even harder, she squeezed back, the pressure too much to keep inside her own skin. It flowed into him in jagged, painful pieces, even if she miraculously kept her voice steady.

"Someone was out of place, or in the wrong place at the wrong time and he almost got caught. Those details are kind of blurry now," she said. "I remember we had to move fast, so very fast to get out of there that I almost crashed several times. By some miracle, I kept us on the road. But then there were the railroad tracks that I...didn't take properly. We were going too fast. I hit them too hard."

Entwined against his darker skin, her knuckles glowed pale, like bones patterning his flesh. She swallowed the shame, inch by burning inch, but it was still everywhere. "Later, at the hospital, long after they'd stabilized me, long after they'd told me Keira hadn't survived, Jerrod finally showed his face. I knew then that there was no going back for us. I guess I'd known it for a while, but none of that mattered once I was determined to make a life for my child."

"Summer...I can't imagine—I'm so sorry," Reyes whispered. He angled his body around hers, like he could physically shield her from the past, from the sorrow that had eclipsed all else for too long. "It's not your fault."

She allowed herself to absorb the feel of him for a few, supported moments then straightened to look at him straight on. "You're wrong about that. It was my fault, and I'll keep that destruction and death with me for the rest of my life."

"No," he asserted. "Despite what you may think, I do understand pain and death better than most. I understand how debilitating misplaced guilt can be, growing like a virus and eating you alive. It makes living with it feel unbearable. It's like being continuously consumed. I know what it feels like when living, existing, feels undeserved while the person who should be is not."

Slowly, she realized he was speaking of his father and saw a shadowy mirror of similar torment reflecting back at her when his eyes met hers. He did know, better than many could. "You go to such great lengths not to feel, to shut it all down, lock it all away…I know what that necessity is like."

"I know but you figured out a way to break me open, to make me feel," she said, awareness sharp. The next came out like a dare. "Yet you don't offer me the same. You tell me to lean on you, to trust you, but with no reciprocation."

He hardened like stone, confirmation of her failed attempt of incitement. "*You* never would have told me if that bastard hadn't expressed his fucking apathy, the fucking inhumane—" He spoke so coldly, accusatorially, like ice stabbing her skin.

"I—"

"No. I never would have known anything—your

reasoning, your pain—had it not been for Metzinger's total lack of humanity just now. You would have kept me comfortably in the dark."

What right did he have to be so mad at her own affliction? To wield an elemental fury beneath all this frost? "You hypocrite," she let loose a painful hiss.

It hurt to look at him, after all the warmth, all the support he'd just shown. "That is so messed up. You don't tell me anything and I'm supposed to strip myself bare? Lay it all out on the table? Admit that, after everything I did for my sister, after all the bad stuff, that it had to take the death my child to get me to stop? You have no right to judge me. No right to look at any decision I made, ripped to pieces, forced to choose between cancer and lost motherhood. But no," she kept going, cathartic release purging out of her. "I'm nearly done feeling sorry for myself. If circumstances hadn't been what they were, had I not been made to face impossible decisions, I never would have begun to face all the ugly parts of myself. The selfish parts, the parts that make me rage, the parts that make me want to curl up, give up. I'm not the person I was and I'm not sure who I am now, but at least I can tell you the person I'm *trying* to be is better than who came before all this."

He drew a hand down his face, exasperation clear. "You're right, Summer, I'm sorry. I'll try not to judge what I don't understand. But I admit that I don't completely. I don't understand your lack of disclosure, not at this point. Not with me…"

She shifted her shoulders. "So be it then. I'm used to being misunderstood."

"Summer, please."

Refusing to look at the hurt she detected in the way

his arms flexed across his chest, shoulders bunching, she reminded herself how they would never have stood a chance. But she also never thought he would plead her name. Never thought he would feel matched anger or something parallel to grief over her past.

Accepting this, he pivoted as if she hadn't just told him about losing Kiera, as if he hadn't just begged for…what she couldn't give. "With the new information about Metzinger and tracking cars on campus, I don't know when I'll be back."

His tone was quiet, punctuated with pristine professionalism. If she detected his storm beneath, he hid it so well, wrapping it in layers of carefully forged ice. "Until Jenkins is brought up to speed, the monitoring of Five Star will continue, especially if he feels that Metzinger is leading us in conflicting directions."

She nodded. "You're leaving. Again."

Turning away, Reyes looked around slowly, as though he was visually mapping her home, like he didn't have plans to return. "I'm leaving."

"Do you have…somewhere else to go when you're not with the team, I mean?" Unwarranted worry mingled with something else sharp. Did envy have her boring holes into his back before he finished his visual sweep?

"When I need sleep, I'll head home."

"Home?"

"I have a place out toward St. Simon's, not too far."

"St. Simon's…you're a local. You live here. Near Savannah." Each sentence was short, abbreviated as if it would help her process the information into easier, non-threatening chunks. He was facing her way again and his conflict was not as well concealed as she'd first thought. "You stayed here anyway?" She couldn't keep the accusation out of her voice. Foolishly, it still hurt, the many, many layers of his nondisclosure.

"When I proposed that I take up residence here, to a degree, while you were in the field, we seemed to come to a mutual understanding about it. I did it to make things flow better on a larger scale. Which it did."

"Did it now?"

Hurt rose up on self-righteous spires, ones that raged about being used, being manipulated by yet another male who thought they knew better than she. For unexplainable reasons, she fought to keep the temper contained. "I would have kept fighting you off until you'd left if I had known it was negotiable, but you threatened me, made me think it would have to be this way."

"I did. And I would do it again if I had to." He spoke without remorse. "If it meant being here for you, doing what was best…"

"The best for you, maybe. Do you have any idea what this mayhem has done to *me*? Everything I've gone though, even with you?"

"You *know* I do," an echo of that swirling storm lashed into his voice. "It's why I'm here, to help you get through this and bring everything to its rightful outcome. It's the only way you can get completely free."

"What if that rightful outcome had resulted in my prosecution? If you had found out earlier that my hands were even dirtier than you originally thought? No, exactly, don't answer that, I already know. Just like now you'll go, because it's what's best for the *outcome*."

"I'll do what I have to do, don't you know how heartless I am? How calculating, how cold?" He prowled back over to her, losing his grip on the emotions he'd reined back in tight. "Don't you know how easy it is for me to use people, manipulate situations without giving a single damn about their wellbeing? Why do you think I'm single? Why I don't waste time with a partner, a significant other? It's all about choices."

His scent, his breath invaded everywhere, all at once. She wanted to take a step back, break the rapture of his hold over her, just by being so close.

"You're...you're not like that."

"No?" he smiled grimly. "It's irrelevant that you know a single thing about me. It's detrimental, in fact, if you do."

"But I do know, Liam," she spoke his name on a hush of air, then amended, "I know some things, I know...you. You have amazing self-control. You only told me that stuff about your family because you were trying to get me to—"

"Wouldn't it be nice if that was the truth? If I did possess some amount of self-control when I'm around you, if I didn't lose my mind every time, I came this close." He pressed his face into her neck, inhaling deeply. Her fingers trembled to reach up, to touch him but she was no longer sure it would be welcome.

"Just when I tell you that you lock everything up so carefully, you accuse me of the same. But you break me open. You make me feel...everything."

Her heart shuddered as his arms snaked around her. A hand gently slid up to cradle the back of her skull in exquisite contrast. But even if her heart responded to his, a reflection to his own confession, her mind processed that his embrace held a finality.

The withdrawal stole fractures of that heart, ones which had only just begun to fuse again. She knew he had more to say about the case. And when he dropped his hands entirely, her suspicions proved true.

"Your situation can only end when we produce undeniable results. As in Metzinger himself. No associates or substitutions. Only then will you be free. I'll accept nothing less."

"It's not really up to you, how this plays out. But thank you."

"Don't thank me. Damn it, don't thank me for something that's already what you deserve. You are more than all this."

Then softer, so soft Summer thought she might have simply willed the words into existence. "Just like you're more than your past, more than your pain."

Her phone vibrated on the counter next to where he stood, resulting in a pivotal glance down. If he had planned on just handing it over, it never made it because he stared hard at the screen for multiple moments, attention caught and not in a good way.

"That number...Do you know who this is?" she asked.

He turned the phone with his fingertips so she could see the familiar yet unknown number. With a nod from her, Reyes clicked on the message.

—Meet me at the waterfront if you want to keep your freedom. East entrance to the boardwalk—

His mouth was hard, eyes glittering. "How long has this number been contacting you?"

Like she was somehow responsible for this person's actions, Summer flicked her gaze from his face to the screen and back. "Look," she gestured, a bit desperately, no longer wanted to hide. "You can see the history...how long it's been going on."

"Which has been a little while, hasn't it?"

Affirming his suspicions with a scroll, Reyes' face flattened into impassible steel. It was difficult to look at him when he could look at her in such a way.

"Please, I'm sorry. I should have told you from the beginning when whoever it is started sending them. There's been a few different numbers like that, but all with seven or eight at the end."

Needing to erase the awful, hard expression he wore, she added, "I just thought it was Jerrod harassing me, which wouldn't be a huge deal."

"Not a huge deal?" he repeated softly, dangerously.

"I mean disturbing, but it's happened before. And now with you involved, the FBI knows about him...it's not like I had somewhere else to take this, to report him. Authorities are here, right now, trying to take him down."

"Summer," his eyes were so dark, the hue was haunting, "Don't even think about going down to Bay Street." When it sounded like he wanted to say more, when that steel softened a bit, he turned. "I've got to go."

"Wait," she cried as he swiped up his jacket, heading for the door. "Do you know something about this? Do you know *who* this is?"

"Promise me," he growled, one hand ready to yank the door from its hinges while the other coiled into a fist. "Promise me you will wait here until you hear from me."

"Okay, Liam," she held his stare, "I won't go."

****

The next few hours crept by. Sleep came in fits and spurts, never restful, always on the surface. As if her body was prepared to leap into action at any moment, yet there was nowhere to go, nothing to do. A kaleidoscope of scenarios afflicted her, running on relentless loops. Every time she was jostled awake again, they would pick up where they'd left off before sleep afforded only a brief reprieve.

Why would Jerrod target someone like Ayana? Was it as simple as her connection to the college that he made it out to be? Or was he angling for something deeper, more sinister? Was it arrogant to think his angle had something to do with her in the first place? After all, it was *her* office assistant he'd recruited.

Had it been safer to assume the unknown numbers were just from Jerrod, or at least, an extension of his reach? Someone he was using to make a point. She could admit that she had chosen to think that, keeping the harassment more easily boxed away as just one more egregious action taken by her ex.

Reyes thought otherwise...

Something about the texts had triggered a reaction beyond the obvious. Reyes knew something else, or suspected something else, and was choosing to keep it to himself. She wouldn't beg for his confidence, wouldn't reduce herself to desperation to gain his disclosure. Despite that, she wished he would choose to tell her. Would choose to reveal his thoughts, his feelings.

Even if he didn't, she had every intention of keeping her promise—right up until her brain rationalized all the reasons why she *shouldn't*.

Summer tried pulling each thought apart to analyze, attaching it to something reasonable, something solid. But all the unknowns and uncertainties equated to trying to hold onto a butterfly.

To no avail.

By the time the next message came through,

morning light had fully established that she could get no more rest. Still, the sender of the request surprised her yet again, enough that she was up and dressed and out the door, if only to finally bring this whole thing to its reckoning.

Chapter Twenty-One

Despite the light and the warmth her apartment offered on the new day, Jerrod's cold sanctuary lay shrouded in shadow.

With the window coverings drawn, the ornate qualities of his wealth became less obtuse and more eerie. Perhaps that was the cause of the ominous misgivings rolling through her stomach. But if it were just the environment, not the occupant, Summer doubted she'd feel quite so much like she'd thrown herself into an irreversibly dire situation. She should have learned from the last time she'd done this.

Jerrod sat at the island, a vortex of negative energy amidst the sea of cold stone. There were no spreads of food or chilled wine, either for extravagance or bribery. No, he sat alone, waiting, causing her creeping fear to start clanging harder. And she'd come unprepared, no strategy, no insight. No angle offered from Liam on how best to navigate the situation.

"Morning, Summer. Sleep okay?" The inquiry sounded mundane, innocuous, if it hadn't come from the mouth of someone who had, just mere hours ago, expressed a lack of regret over their pregnancy loss.

"Mmhmm," she managed, letting the sound sway whichever way he wanted to hear. Did he want her disheveled, broken down and desolated from grief? Or did he expect her to shed their previous discussion like a snake shedding what no longer fit? Whichever way his mood ran, she hoped she could match the right response.

When he didn't motion for her to join him, she felt like this had already begun to spiral down fast. Even if he had beckoned for her, she couldn't get her legs to cooperate further than the edge of tiles delineating the kitchen. Like a magnet repelling its identical side, it felt impossible to wade through the opposition and break the repulsion.

Intuition warned her to pinch her tongue, to lock her lips but Summer found that while her lower half didn't want to kick into gear, her mouth had other plans. "Why haven't you hit the tow yard? I got you access, I know you have people on the ready. Why are you waiting?" Resentment percolated into the already nasty mix of reactions assaulting her insides. If only she could keep her face stoic, unaffected.

Lazily, he rolled his head back and forth a bit, feigning to relieve stiff muscles. With hands sliding up to link behind the back of his neck, fingers hooking and elbows splaying, he leaned back dramatically and leveled her with a look full of disdain. "The tow yard is a sham."

"A sham?"

"Yes. A trick, a game, nothing more."

"A game? Who are you playing?"

But she already knew who. Already knew why her senses were straining.

Disdain shifted into slow victory, as though the game had already been won, officially or otherwise. "You, Summer. I'm playing you, just like you've been playing me. Hell of a bluff, I'll give you that. Now why, exactly, you've come crawling back in here, putting up this much of a front—that's the real question. Unfortunately, now may not be the time to dig down quite as deep to the truth of the matter as much as I'd like. There's always later, however, and I've got a feeling whatever's wound you up to think you could pull this one over has to be very interesting indeed. But perhaps," he added cryptically, "After this all goes down, it won't matter so much."

She felt the ground shift dangerously beneath her feet. No matter where she maneuvered, no matter how much she rebalanced, she *would* be caught in this round of crossfire. He was gaining dark pleasure from watching her crack, from knowing she knew there was no longer a way out for her.

Just as she was scrambling for something, anything, that might shield the fallout, Katelyn walked into the room.

If her shock had gravity, she would be on her knees, tethered low.

Slowly, slowly, Summer's widened eyes slid between the two, trying and failing to fathom a reason, any reason, why her sister was here. Why her sister was looking at her like at any moment she might be sick. Why Jerrod, although smug, had an impossible slice of pity cross his face as he watched them both assess one another.

"Katelyn. What are you *doing* here?" The question, the demand, was barely above a whisper but Summer felt the rush of trepidation all the way to the tips of her toes.

"I can answer your question," Jerrod eventually offered when it appeared that Katelyn wasn't going to. No, her sister appeared overtly ill, her physical presence diminished to the point where old habits pushed at

Summer to go help, to go assist.

But she waited, spine rigid. Waiting to hear why, two people who never deigned to take much interest in one another while they were in-laws, let alone after the demise, would be together now. Just as Jerrod had uncovered the truth about her, just as everything was about to implode.

"Your sister asked to come, to get you here and clear the air. There're some things you two need to talk about."

"Jerrod, I—"

"I know, Summer, much more than you think. This little...reunion, it never would have worked out between us. You and I are on *vastly* different pages, like I said. And right now, until we can reconvene again, there's somewhere I need to be."

Then with a gallant little wave of his hand, he announced, "I'm out. Reset the lock button behind you."

Wait, she thought, nerves flaring. This isn't what's supposed to happen. She was supposed to see this through, get him to the tow yard and securely into the FBI's clutches. She was supposed to be set free. This wasn't why she had come, not when she'd thought that an opportunity to send him to his reckoning was truly within reach.

All the possible outcomes disintegrated into ashes as she watched her ex-husband skirt around Katelyn like she wasn't even there. Desperation was a living thing, thrashing, clawing wings begging to escape the inevitable.

Then, as he passed, he shot a look back at her sister before dropping his head beside her ear. "I figured you deserved to know. After everything."

Only once she was sure they were alone, engulfed

by the silence of the house did she cut her eyes back to Katelyn, panicked sorrow swelling in her chest. Because whatever Jerrod felt like she deserved to know was still a pale comparison to her past deceit.

"Katelyn," she tried, before raising then dropping her hands helplessly at her sides. These confessions were heavy, leaden things, piling up behind her teeth. They could stay contained no longer even if she had no clue how to articulate their release. "I'm sorry. So sorry. I've been lying to you, about a lot—including Jerrod—but I think you must have known that, knew something was off and now the FBI's involved and—"

"Summer. Stop." Katelyn's command held a breathy, fleeting quality, yet silenced her.

Summer absorbed the fragility of her sister's folded limbs, the sunken quality of her cheeks. Had it only been a few weeks since she'd last seen her? Since she'd looked so vital and healthy when they'd been out with Mom. This person before her was a shadow of herself, scaring her beyond whatever frightening possibility had brought them to this moment right here.

Katelyn straightened up a little, met her eyes with a level of conviction, "I'm the reason."

"The reason for what?"

"The reason for all of this. The reason you got tangled up with Jerrod in the first place. I'm the reason why you're here now."

"I know you asked me to come but...how can that be true?"

Shock waves started to ripple, causing little trembles to drop deep into the pit of her stomach. Nothing about this was right. An aberration of the reality she knew, even if that reality was riddled with her own guilt.

"It is true," her sister asserted more firmly this time. "I'm the one who set that whole night up, the night we went out. Me and Gabe, we knew who he was, knew what he did."

The waves of shock increased their strength, nearly causing the pressure in her abdomen to buckle her. "You set me up? With Jerrod?"

"Summer, we knew all of it, all about what Jerrod did—what he does—and we still gave you to the wolf."

Chapter Twenty-Two

There had been a dark period, after she was alone, truly alone, when she'd experienced episodes of dissociation. It terrified her afterwards, as though the pain she carried from the loss of Kiera, the loss of her marriage, could only mean something if it kept on surviving. If the wounds stayed open, stayed sharp, then everything was still real.

As Summer absorbed the blow, numbness began to creep up her spine, marching up to battle the din roaring inside her mind. Separation could be sweet relief, from the cause of the person standing in front of her, wilting before her eyes. The one she'd sacrificed for, broken laws for. Hidden the ugliness from, except, she was the one to know all along.

Summer didn't want relief. She wanted truth. "You've known? This whole time, you've known...everything?"

Katelyn repositioned herself, using the granite slab as support against her hip. "I didn't know the FBI had caught up to him, or that you have been somehow working for them." Confusion crossed her face, coupled with that shrinking sadness. "You're safe from it, though? You're not who they're after?"

Bitter laughter bubbled up her throat. "Safe is relative. There's nothing safe about any of this. If I don't produce what I'm told to produce, my fate is as good as

Jerrod's."

Flickers of outrage pierced through the shock, scattering the numbness that bloomed in her bones. "You *knew*," Summer released the bitter accusation, welcoming in the heat of anger, letting it shield her suffering. "You knew about Jerrod, you knew what he does, what he's like. You...and your fucking husband?"

"Yes," Katelyn agreed softly. "We knew what Jerrod did hidden behind EarthScapes. Gabe was an acquaintance, from long ago. But never one who could cross over into his inner circle."

"And that was a thought? An intention? To actually enter into his dealings on purpose?" She struggled to find logic, to find sense, but the facts challenged everything she knew. Everything she thought was real and true and good about Katelyn. "*Why?*" A wealth of despair punctuated the question.

"The cancer," Katelyn bit out tersely. "It's always been all about this fucking cancer." She swept her hand angrily down her torso. "And we needed a way to get money. A lot of it and fast. I couldn't sacrifice my physical state so we needed someone else who could."

"*You* couldn't sacrifice?" She had experienced betrayal, more than once, but betrayal by family, by Katelyn, obliterated her heart. "You couldn't, so you sacrificed me to do the dirty work. Sacrificed me to get you what you needed because you and Gabe couldn't be *inconvenienced*, is that it? Stealing, lying, laundering, that's all nothing to you?"

She saw Katelyn flinch as she lashed out each of the crimes committed in the name of obligation, of love, of duty, but she kept going. "Everything I went through with Jerrod...with Kiera. It was because *you* couldn't

231

take the risk. You and your worthless husband."

"Summer, please, I'm heartbroken over your miscarriage, you must know that."

"I know nothing," she leveled lowly, earning a deepening look of despair.

"And I am so sorry about how Jerrod treated you in the end," Katelyn persisted. "At first, he was charismatic and you two were inseparable for a while, so I thought maybe you had found something genuinely good, even with all the bad. I swear to God, I didn't know you laundered anything."

"That's your ethical line? Not committing a federal crime? Don't you fucking judge me. I would have done anything to help you, and I did! For a long time. Do you honestly think Jerrod just gave those kinds of handouts whenever I needed him to? No. I had to protect the money, hide it, stash it. Keep it ready so *you* could use it when you needed it."

Summer needed to move, needed to shift the rage she now felt pooling vicious acid in her stomach, making her want to puke. This was what Jerrod thought she deserved to know—that her sister, not him, was the original conspirator. That wasn't entirely true either, but her brain fought to unravel all the nasty, complicated threads of the individual roles being played, all while she'd been left in the dark, a target to be used and manipulated.

"Did Jerrod know your angle from the beginning too? Did he just play along, for who knows what sick satisfaction? Damn it, I can't do this…" Everything was growing more jumbled, contorting and twisting to fit this horrible new paradigm.

"No, he didn't have anything to do with our plan in

the beginning. He knows who Gabe is but not what we were after. Your relationship evolved authentically."

"Why should I believe that?"

"I guess you can take my word or not," Katelyn sighed heavily. "But everything I'm saying now is the truth. He didn't know. Your connection with him was genuine."

"I don't know if that makes this better or worse. But I do know that if you would have just asked me for help, told me what was going on, no matter how dire, I would have still helped you however I could."

"I know. I know that, Summer, but it doesn't matter now because I'm not hiding the fact that I might have still made the same choice, even after everything. I needed to…save myself."

"And have you been saved?" she snarled. "Has it all been eradicated while I've been tied up with the FBI's threats? You say you've been getting treatment but is that just another ruse? Another lie?"

"The cancer's still there, it's not a lie. I have been getting treatments."

"And the money now? Where do you get it?"

Face ashen, Katelyn shuddered a breath, "We'll work it out somehow. There will be a way. A legal way."

"Then it doesn't sound like, after everything's been said and done, that you got a savior after all."

"I know, Summer, and I'll pay the price. Forgive me."

And with that final exertion, Katelyn crumpled to the ground.

****

A vicious debate ensued for the few critical moments while Katelyn was incapacitated.

Those moments were achingly slow, as though suspended in time, unbound by reality. Even a few hours ago, the choice would have been quite clear, and Summer knew she wouldn't have hesitated in the slightest. But those critical moments thrown in at pivotal times, those that truly matter, make all the difference.

Her phone was gripped in her hand like a weapon as she studied her sister's position on the floor. Chest rising rapidly, eyes roving as she tried to dignify herself, it was clear that while cognizant, her ability to command her body was severely diminished.

It was probably the most honest depiction she'd witnessed of Katelyn. Stripped away was the presumption, the need to prove her stamina. And now, thanks to Jerrod's intervention, the truth finally exposed. He had done something decent, something she never believed him capable of doing. And she knew she held his fate, as well as Katelyn's, in her hands. It had always been so, ever since Reyes had darkened her doorstep. So why now did everything suddenly feel so undeserved?

There was nothing fair, or right, or just about any of it. The selfish side of her that sought vengeful emancipation from the old attachments still wreaking havoc felt wronged all over again. Shorted of a clean break, of a rightful reckoning.

"Just do it already."

Her sister's voice was jagged and thready, slicing through the silence.

"Do what?"

"Make the call and be done. Get your freedom, you deserve it. You have my word that I will admit to my involvement and give whatever statement is needed."

Triggered into action by Katelyn's words, Summer

knelt to help reposition her so that her back was propped against the island cabinet. That simple act of support softened her, muting the sharpness, just from the physical touch.

Time was of the essence now. If she sounded the alarm and they got there fast enough, that freedom could be attained. Shutting down the spinning in her head, Summer stepped out of ear shot, relaying what she knew, doing what she could.

Upon returning to the kitchen, Summer sat down beside her sister, experiencing a chasm widening between them, mapped by undefinable, unfathomable lines.

Eventually she found words again. Quieter, less angry ones that could span the separation. But painful nonetheless.

"I'd ask you why you want to work at the clinic now, after everything that's happened but I'm really afraid of that answer. Did you know about Ayana too?"

If Katelyn was surprised by the question, she didn't show it, only sucked in air like it could give her renewed life. "I knew he was interested in her, but I didn't know why. We had crossed paths when you started training me, I assume that was when he was targeting her as a potential addition." Katelyn paused to inhale again, shutting her eyes for a moment. "Me working at the clinic, it's been a chance to try to make things right, to try and do it a different way. Nothing more to it than that."

When Summer didn't respond, she murmured, "But you don't trust that either."

"It's not that I think you're trying to lie to me right now, I just…it's too much to work through here. I need time."

"I know, and I'm sorry."

She let her knuckles brush the back of her sister's hand but didn't say anything more. Summer wasn't entirely sure how long they sat there in the time warp but eventually muffled voices giving curt commands found their way in. She felt the moment Katelyn realized they weren't alone by the way she tensed, bracing for a battle that had already been lost.

Because it wasn't the FBI that entered the kitchen but several paramedics.

"I thought you called for help," Katelyn said.

"I did. This is the help that's needed."

A flash of disappointment washed over her features as she stared at Summer. Then she closed her eyes, gave in and allowed the first responders to load her onto the stretcher.

Summer stood but made no move to follow. She watched the efficiency of the transport in reserved silence. Right up until the lone agent walked in behind the medical personnel.

She steeled herself as she faced the new arrival. "Where's Liam?"

Eyes sharp, the agent regarded Summer intently. "*Agent* Reyes implored me to come tell you we got him."

"*Him?* Meaning, Jerrod?"

A ghost of a smirk crossed her lips, one that hardly qualified as friendly. "Yeah, we got Metzinger."

Chapter Twenty-Three

A month later

The townhouse lay deathly quiet while Summer brewed tea.

Meticulously, she measured leaves before situating the strainer into the mug. Waited for her kettle to heat. Watched until bubbles began to pop up against the glass, gentle at first but growing angrier beneath the element.

It had been quite a while since her movements were this unhurried, though her fingers still ached and itched for productivity. A self-imposed break after weeks of blurred, frenzied activity seemed a necessity at the time, to not think, to not feel. To be able to address responsibilities without letting emotions take control or take her down.

But she was putting an end to that luxury.

There were matters to face that could only be effectively dealt with head on, not while she was purposefully distracting herself with work to avoid her head ruminating down into a dark, toxic spiral.

Self-awareness was the first savior and only after enough time had passed, enough distance had spanned, did she allow herself the time needed to let the spiral take hold. The only way to get through it was to go through.

Her clients would keep until she reopened by week's end. With Katelyn still weak and Ayana consulting a lawyer, there was no avenue for extra support. Her mom had kindly offered hers, but she'd declined.

Emily could go where she was needed most—to sit by her daughter's side while Summer tended to the tatters of her heart. And if Ayana succeeded in untangling herself from the mess she'd slid into, Summer doubted she would resume her role at Longtime Sun. *She* wasn't sure she would even allow it, no matter how gracious she tried to be.

Claiming innocence over the accusations, Ayana held strong in her denials about being chosen specifically to spy on Summer. The students' cars came as an unexpected bonus.

But solving her work problems wasn't the reason for the hiatus and Summer reminded herself those issues would be dealt with as well, because she was nothing if not diligent in finding resolutions. The only fault with her problem solving in a different area was that she simply didn't have enough information to resolve...anything.

Reyes, much like the version of herself right before reality faltered in Jerrod's kitchen, had vanished. Everyone had. The last person of authority to offer her the decency of communication had been the agent who'd come to report while they'd led Katelyn away that Jerrod was now in custody. Since then, there had been nothing. No calls. No anonymous texts. Silence. And she'd also done little to close the gap in reverse, allowing the powers at play to dismiss her so easily after using her so callously. If they ignored her, then she wasn't being charged. Yet.

Summer removed the steeping leaves, and gripping the mug with both hands, moved over to the window to let the late autumn sun slide waning heat into her bones.

Between the tea and the light, she felt less chilled, though she knew the source of her cold went far deeper than where any of those things could truly reach. She stood in forced stillness, intentional silence. When the floorboards eventually began to creak, she merely assumed the old place had no more tolerance for inactivity than she did. Meditation was not her strong suit.

But when they echoed a pattern, like footsteps following, Summer turned to see Reyes, dressed like a civilian, crossing her living room. The hands on her mug tightened. Afraid to add any inflection that would betray her astonishment, she spoke flatly, "I wouldn't have thought you'd still have your key. Sloppy of me to not have the locks changed."

"Very. But since you didn't get around to it, I figured I'd make use of what was still in my possession."

She wasn't ready to do this, she realized too late. Her hands trembled as she set her mug down, the dregs having gone cold. The warmth she'd acquired fled just as hastily, no longer able to offer any comfort. "What are you doing here?"

Maybe if she was direct, he would be as well, and they could both get this part over. For a person who claimed to thrive on integrity, on accomplishments, for someone who didn't avoid conflict, Summer hadn't thought ghosting was in his repertoire. How wrong she'd been.

"I have news which I rightly assumed has not been shared with you yet."

So, it was business. Nothing more. "You're right. No one shared any news. In fact, no one's talked to me in weeks. Not anyone, not you…"

Stopping the line to accusation, she pressed her lips together, willing herself to be as unaffected as he was showing. He had updates, surely she could listen to what he needed to say without interjecting her grievances. She certainly didn't expect the look of remorse that glanced across his face to make her question herself all over again.

"You've officially gotten your fresh start."

"They granted me immunity?"

"They granted you immunity," he confirmed.

"And Katelyn?" she asked, slipping the question into the pause that followed, like he knew she would inquire.

"Her role in Metzinger's trial remains undetermined. When she will be called to testify is currently contingent on her health status and when a doctor releases her."

"I know she told you all that it was her interference alone. She covered for Gabe, took full responsibility so he didn't have to be involved. She shouldn't have done that."

"Whether or not she should have, she did and as of now, he's not a part of this. If they're able to trace anything back to him though, that could turn the tides...or if you come forward with what you know. You are aware that you will still need to give your testimony?"

"Yes, but I don't know what Gabe has actually done, other than what Katelyn confessed and...I can't do it. She's made her choice and if something is found that incriminates Gabe, so be it. But it won't be my implication that does it."

"I understand." When she raised a brow, he smiled,

"You know I do, even if you don't want to admit it."

It almost made her smile in return. His smugness, the natural arrogance, that had antagonized yet intrigued her from the beginning, was back in force. Despite everything that lay unfinished, his flash of levity eased the cold a little, adding a layer of warmth which had eluded her for a month.

"I don't even know how things ended," she said quietly. "With Jerrod. With all the rest." She hadn't meant to go there, didn't want to ask where he'd been if he didn't want to share it. It could only mean something if he chose to tell it on his own.

"We were able to intercept him in the student lot, just as you'd reported. Thanks to your quick actions, I left the waterfront with enough time to pull a few guys off the Five Star lot and take Metzinger into custody. And don't, for one moment, feel remorse about what you did."

"What makes you think I feel remorseful about doing what needed to be done?"

"Like I said, your face, much like the rest of you," he moved closer, raking his gaze over her, "shows all the emotions. Sadness, guilt. Passion. All that fire."

Summer felt it flame up, just having him look at her that way. Hearing him say it out loud, the truth about all the things she felt so intensely. She needed to own it. They were all parts of her, not all of them pliable or pretty.

"He didn't have to do what he did, with Katelyn. By facilitating her confession, I can acknowledge that his morality in that moment makes me regret how things had to end, but I don't, for one minute, wish I could take it back. If I hadn't warned you, if he hadn't told me, then I never would have been able to return to my life. Even if I don't understand why he would give himself away. He knew of my deception, to some degree."

"That we may never know. Maybe you were a greater weakness to him than he ever let on."

"If such a thing were true, I still wouldn't do things differently."

"Good to hear. You deserve to have a choice that's entirely yours, whatever it is you want to do next. No matter how his case, or Katelyn's, travels through the courts, you won't be a part of it anymore—unless you want to be."

She breathed deeply, feeling freedom burst free inside of her chest as she wondered at his words. A choice. Her choice. What would his be now that this was done?

"Wait a sec." She backtracked, realizing what else he'd revealed. "You were at the waterfront? Not Five Star?"

"Your text threats needed to be dealt with. But that's finished now too. It won't be an issue anymore."

"You got to give me more than that, Liam. Please."

He turned slightly away, causing a tremor of fear to tick in her chest. But she couldn't make him choose. Then, he sighed, just audibly, as if he were only now coming to terms with the choice himself. "I know."

Gesturing towards his clothes, he added a little shrug and smiled, "I'll have a lot more to give you now that I've got more time on my hands."

"What do you mean?"

"I tendered my resignation, effective immediately."

Summer stared at him. "You left the FBI?"

"I did. For a lot of reasons. But the main one was

that it was Jenkins who was messing with you. My fucking boss decided to try and take you down, sabotage the assignment, because of me."

She hadn't expected another bombshell to land at her feet, especially one involving a person she'd never laid eyes on. "When I saw him waiting for you, like he figured he had this thing in the bag," Reyes went on, "I took pictures, got the evidence, right before you told me to go to the student lots. It was enough to put the pressure on him to release me from the task force and still keep my law enforcement credentials."

Pressing fingers to her brows, she shook her head in disbelieve. "Hold on, you gave up your career because someone tried to extort me? He must have known about the laundering then and I don't see what that has to do with you.

"When I confronted him after Metzinger's take down, he didn't say he knew about it, but it's kind of safe to assume he found out somehow. Denied everything though and told me I had no proof that would stand up, then proceeded to accept my request for dismissal with only a little more…convincing."

"You can be very convincing," she conceded, which earned her a grin. "He could be right, though, if he pushes that you have no proof. Definitely circumstantial."

"He could, but I don't think he'll bring that kind of investigation down upon himself. He's had a lot to prove since I've been working with him, always feeling threatened by another's success. He was attempting to take out what he viewed as competition, even though I had no designs on his job."

"You suspected it was someone on the inside when

you saw the texts, didn't you? For you to have gone down there, to pursue what could have been a dead end…"

"The burner phones we use populate with the seven, eight combo, so that also wouldn't bode so well for him. But in some ways, I'm grateful for the kick in the ass. I want to be done. My motivations…have changed."

When she thought he would stop there, he surprised her. "It was never going to end well for me, when my reasons for being there were completely vengeful. I started to realize that my father wouldn't want me to go out that way, doing something spiteful that I would come to regret. Better to move on and cut my losses. Which, really, are only a few."

Processing all of what he'd said, all the change brought with it, Summer ventured, "What are you going to do now?"

"That's a great question. And I guess it all depends."

"Depends on what?"

"On you."

With that, he drew out his phone, turned it so she could see the flight information.

"You're planning a trip to Bali?"

"I've never been to Asia before." He slowly pulled the phone back. "And, if I recall, neither have you."

Butterfly nerves tickled her stomach, a replay of one of their earliest conversations running a reel through her mind. "No," she said carefully, "Never been."

"I figured I needed to ask you which dates would be best for the clinic, when you'd be willing to shut the doors for a few days, even though I suspect you'll tell me that no days are good days for that."

"You're right about that but sometimes it's a

necessity…is this—you want me to go with you?"

Reaching up to frame her face with his hands, he trailed his thumbs along her jaw line before tucking a few strands of hair behind her ears. "I'm asking if you'll go with me. We could get to discussing all those things I owe you more transparency about. And take a breather, a break away from here before you come back to deal with the heavy stuff with your sister and the trial."

Nodding, she turned her cheek into his hand, breathing in his scent. "You've been gone a long time…you just left and didn't say anything. Didn't tell me why."

His hands tightened slightly before coming to trace the line of her collarbones on their journey down to grip her fingers tightly with his. "I'm sorry. I had to make sure my plan with Jenkins would work, that he would be open to my negotiation. And then…I didn't know if you would want to see me again once it was all over."

"You put me through a lot."

"I did. I had to. It's what makes me good at my job but bad at a lot of other stuff. Maybe a clean slate would be better."

He looked down and away, and never had Summer seen him look so unsure of himself. To risk showing his feelings for her, unguarded, an honest indication of how harmful her rejection of him would be.

"Then I guess it's a good thing you just said that my life is back to being my choice again. So, I'll decide how I spend my time. And with whom, clean slate be damned."

She laughed with genuine reverence when his head lifted in pure surprise, joy blooming brightly. Sliding his arms around her waist, he matched her reverent look, like he hadn't fully trusted she'd come back around to him.

"You sure about that? I mean, this isn't exactly how I thought things would turn out, career hiatus at thirty-four, a fair amount of regret to work through."

"Only as long as you're sure you want to deal with a divorced woman who has a criminal record and jabs needles into people for a living. Not to mention my own amount of unresolve conflict to process."

"It sounds to me like we're an even match."

Fear and joy were equally raw and real. She didn't want the fear to win but it lived inside of her along with the happiness. By acknowledging it, she felt more courageous, enough to take the chance. Something she never thought was possible a year or two ago.

"November."

When he shot her a questioning look, she took a deep breath. "Late November is good for the clinic, before we contend with more travelers for the holidays."

"That's only a little way off."

"Then I think we should get planning."

His arms wrapped her up in a crushing hug that had her feeling the weight of that tired, predictable armor falling away. Bared to the core, her happiness shone through as she let go, grabbing onto what could be brought back in return.

Mouths meeting, reviving the heat they both coveted, Summer felt the connection in the love and acceptance drowning out the voices of doubt. In their place unfurled something novel, something new—hope for a future that didn't look to undo the pain of the past, but rather to embrace the beauty of true evolution.

A word about the author...

Skye Mueller is the author of thought-provoking fiction, highlighting experiences unique to women that span from joyful and empowering to dark and chaotic.

When she's not writing, she can be found practicing yoga, wandering the beach or cheering on her daughters' athletic pursuits. A Florida native, she resides on the east coast with her husband, 2 children and a trio of pets.

https://skyemueller.com/

www.ingramcontent.com/pod-product-compliance
Lightning Source LLC
Chambersburg PA
CBHW070106030726
47506CB00002B/610